WORTHY

DONNA COONER

Point

Library of Congress Cataloging-in-Publication Data available

ISBN 978-0-545-90393-6

10 9 8 7 6 5 4 3 2 1   17 18 19 20 21

Printed in the U.S.A.   23
First edition, April 2017

Book design by Yaffa Jaskoll

To Aimee. For your editorial skills, enduring patience, and constant kindness.

THE HORNET

Online Forum for Students of Huntsville High School

- You are cordially invited to an **ENCHANTED EVENING**. Huntsville High School's **JUNIOR-SENIOR PROM** will be held on Saturday, April 10. Tickets now on sale in the cafeteria!

- Do you love to write? Are you a Huntsville sophomore or junior? Then you're eligible to enter the 13th Annual Marty Speer Literary Prize for Young Writers contest, presented by the *Thompson Review*, one of the country's most respected literary magazines. If you are the winner or one of the two runners-up, you will see your story published on the *Thompson Review*'s website. In addition, the winner will receive a full scholarship to the *Thompson Review* Young Writers Workshop in Austin, Texas, this summer. Go to martyspeerlitprize.com to enter!

- Congratulations, Kat Lee, SHHS Media Center Aide and the March Hornet Award Winner!

- Are you **WORTHY**? Check out this HOT NEW app just for Huntsville High School students! Everybody's going to be talking about this tomorrow! Don't be left out. Free download *HERE*.

CHAPTER ONE

Shoes can tell you everything about a person. My best friend, Nikki Aquino, says I'm too quick to judge, even though it was a pair of shoes that brought us together in the first place. On the first day of kindergarten, I couldn't stop staring at Nikki's pink glittery high-top sneakers. By lunchtime, she'd convinced me to try them on. She's been convincing me to do things ever since. Today is no exception.

I wait for Nikki by the junior lockers, scrolling through my phone. I open the Hornet, which is our student-run online forum, kind of like a virtual bulletin board where kids can post stuff. The news of the upcoming writing contest makes my stomach jump. My English teacher mentioned that prize yesterday and I'd gotten my hopes up—a chance to go to Austin! My writing published online! But suddenly, I'm nervous. I don't know if I should enter or not. The familiar doubts start to bubble up in my mind. Maybe I'm not good enough.

To distract myself, I click on the link at the bottom of the page. Some potentially stupid new app starts downloading to my phone.

I look up. Still no Nikki.

This after-school meeting was not in my plans and, even though it was all her idea, Nikki is nowhere to be found. I'm not tall enough to see over the top of the crowd so I just wait it out, tapping my red Lucchese cowboy boots—an incredible find at Bobbi's Thrift Shop—against the tiled hallway of Huntsville High School. I lean back against the wall and try not to get swept away by students rushing for the exits.

If I had a superpower, invisibility would definitely be it. Why else would at least ten people bump into me every single day as I walk to and from my classes? When I finally see Nikki waving at me from the end of the hall, I smile in spite of myself.

Unlike me, Nikki walks through the crush of moving bodies with absolute confidence. Nobody jostles her. No one crowds her. In fact, the push of students mystically parts around her and makes way. I don't know how she does it.

Nikki doesn't care if people say a girl her size shouldn't wear leopard-skin tights. *That* is her superpower. Today those tights are tucked into black leather booties that match her size 2X black leather jacket. Nikki calls herself fat without blinking an eye. I call her spectacular.

Unlike Nikki, I'm just average. I have straight, dirty-blonde hair, fair skin, and brown eyes. I'm average height, average weight. And nobody stands out for being average in high school. But being in the middle, blending in, feels comfortable to me. It's like getting into a swimming pool.

I like to walk in slowly from the steps in the shallow end and get used to the water touching my toes, my knees, my waist, my chest. Nikki, of course, always dives in without a moment of hesitation. And sometimes she pulls me in behind her.

Now Nikki stops in front of me, smiling. "You're still coming with me, right?" she asks. She flips her dark hair over one shoulder and narrows her eyes at me. It's a look I know all too well.

I frown and then nod, reluctantly. "Yeah, but I can't stay long. I need to get to work."

"Mrs. Longshore won't care if you're late. Besides, those books are still going to be there no matter when you show up," Nikki says.

My after-school job at the Huntsville Library only pays minimum wage, but at least it's something. And one day I'm going to write one of those books on the shelves. Maybe I'll even come back from wherever famous authors live and put the book up there myself in some kind of big ceremony where everyone claps and asks for my autograph.

It could happen.

But not today, because Nikki is grabbing my arm and pulling me away from the lockers to head to the Junior Prom Planning Committee meeting. Nikki's been on the committee for a month now and she's been begging me to join too. I finally gave in.

"It's our responsibility to help plan the best prom ever," Nikki told me earlier this morning as we walked into school. "When we're seniors, someone is going to be doing all this for us, right?"

Nikki knows what appeals to me. I like to plan. Maybe it was because I was such a fearful child that I became a planner. Most of my childhood was spent afraid of the dark, afraid of bugs, afraid of roller coasters that might make me sick, afraid of dancing and looking like an idiot, afraid of almost everything. But I learned something. If I planned out what was going to happen, with little room for surprise, then I wasn't so afraid.

Proms don't seem as scary as some other things, but it still never hurts to plan.

The one thing I'm *not* planning on is having a date. With no prospects in sight and prom only a few weeks away, I just can't imagine it happening.

I squint down the corridor and sigh. "Okay. Let's get this over with."

"Come on. The meeting is in Mr. Landmann's room," Nikki says, continuing to yank me down the hall toward the history wing.

We make it to the door, but just before we can go inside, Jake Edwards comes up behind Nikki and puts his arms around her, pulling her to his chest. She looks up at him and my heart drops a notch. Not because I'm jealous, but because I'm worried.

This is not a good idea, Nikki.

Nikki and Jake just started dating about a month ago.

I look at them standing side by side. Nikki is a gorgeous, plus-sized Filipina girl with brown skin and thick black hair. Jake looks like a big, blond, blue-eyed Norwegian god or something. They make a striking couple. But Jake is also a star football player and the senior class favorite to be prom king. And he's popular. Much more popular than Nikki.

It makes me nervous.

"Hey, beautiful," he says, kissing Nikki on the forehead and smiling down at her. She smiles back up at him.

He's going to break your heart, Nikki.

"Where are you two going?" Jake asks both of us, but he only looks at Nikki.

I clear my throat. "We have a meeting."

"But I'll see you later?" Jake asks, and Nikki nods, laughing and leaning into his broad chest. She smiles the smile that causes her eyes to crinkle up at the corners and makes her even more beautiful. Sometimes it's hard to be her best friend. She's the sun and I'm Pluto.

I avert my eyes and pull my phone out of my pocket, not wanting to be some kind of third-wheel dork. I see that the new app has finished loading. It's called Worthy, and the icon has a little question mark inside a heart. Weird.

I glance up to see Nikki and Jake kissing. I don't even try to hide my eye roll. I might only be five foot four inches tall, from the top of my messy blonde bun to the tips of my Lucchese boots, but I can throw some shade with the best of them.

"Let's go," I say to Nikki. "We'll be late."

"Bye, Linden," Jake tells me flatly. He knows I don't like him.

Pulling herself away from Jake with one last giggle, Nikki looks back at him over her shoulder, even as she is walking away. He says something I can't hear and she laughs. She has such a great laugh. If he can make her laugh like that, it makes me hope I'm wrong about Jake.

Nikki pulls open the classroom door and pushes me inside. Mr. Landmann glances up from a *King Lear* playbill and cheerfully waves us in. He's the history teacher and the faculty advisor for all things prom, but he's also active in the Huntsville Community Theater. Sometimes his worlds collide. This afternoon, his classroom is filled with more props than students. I look down the rows of desks surrounded by painted cardboard thrones, draped velvet curtains, and life-sized cutouts of various historical figures. *All the world's a stage*, I think. *And I'm just a player. Especially in prom meetings.*

Heather Middleton stands at the front of the room in her knockoff Uggs, trying to get everyone's attention with her perky, high-pitched voice.

"Hey, guys? Everyone?"

No one pays her any attention. Heather is that kid who sits in the front row of every AP class, waving her hand and asking the teacher about extra homework. No one wants to depend on Heather to plan the most glamorous night of our lives, but she always volunteers first.

Jayla Williams, a tall, pretty, African-American girl, sits in the front row. Jayla's captain of our school volleyball team. Today she's painting the fingernails on her right hand bright green, Huntsville High School color, and blowing on her other hand to help it dry faster. She looks up at me and Nikki and waves the finished hand at us in perfect Texas beauty queen style. Jayla is popular. She's one of the Lovelies, as Nikki and I call all the girls in the highest echelon of the popular crowd. She likes Nikki, so by extension she likes me too, I guess.

Nikki and I wave back to Jayla, and then we continue down the aisle to two empty desks. We sit down next to a cardboard cutout of the *Santa Maria*. I twist around to observe the other kids in the room. My writing brain suddenly kicks in—noticing things other people don't. It is hard to turn off.

Max Rossi, junior class president, sits behind Jayla wearing a baseball cap that reads "Real Men Hunt Turkeys" across the front. I can tell by his grin that he is obviously enjoying being the only guy in the room. Max lives across the street from me and we've known each other since we were kids. I also know something about him most people don't. He is highly allergic to strawberries and can't even touch one without breaking out in a painful red rash. I was not above using this special knowledge when we were five and he kept chasing me around the front yard, dangling a giant tree roach in my face. Texas roaches are huge and, if that isn't bad enough, they fly toward you instead of running away from you. I'm terrified of them. So I came up with a plan to deal with Max if it ever happened again. And when it did, I held a baggie full of strawberries over his head until he finally swore never to roach-chase me again.

By the way, I love strawberries. They are like tiny, delicious superheroes.

Max nods toward me when he sees me looking at him, and I quickly glance down at the top of the desk. I still can't believe Max Rossi ended up with the Lovelies. Some things just can't be explained.

The door flies open and Taylor Reed strolls in, carrying a blue-striped Kate Spade bag on one arm. Taylor is the younger sister of last year's prom queen and is definitely one of the Lovelies. She's tall and blonde, with skin the color of those powdered sugar mini-doughnuts. Okay, maybe not that white, but close.

Strawberries? Doughnuts? Great. Now I'm hungry.

I lean across the aisle and ask Nikki, "Do you have a snack?"

She wrinkles up her nose and looks at me like I'm crazy. "A snack? Are we in kindergarten?"

"Sorry," I mutter. I press my hands against my stomach, willing it not to growl.

"Oh. My. God. I'm so late," Taylor announces to the room, then waits a few seconds for a response from the audience, like a great comic waits for the laugh. And, as usuàl, any empty space surrounding Taylor Reed is filled up seamlessly by her adoring fans.

"But we're so glad you made it," Heather says. She stretches out the word *so* several beats for an extra emphasis that goes way beyond her strong Texas accent.

Taylor ignores Heather, making her way down the center aisle. She slides into the empty desk in front of me, then leans over to talk to Jayla and Max.

"Can you believe it? I'm late because I had to go to detention because of all my tardies. Kind of ironic, right?" she drawls.

"Yeah. Crazy," Jayla says, but in a bored tone that tells everyone she couldn't care less if Taylor showed up or not. The rumor is Jayla is going to be Taylor's biggest competition for this year's junior prom queen. Since Taylor is obnoxious, and has at least a couple hundred more followers on social media than any other kid at Huntsville High School, I kind of hope the rumor is right. I always root for the underdog.

Not that Jayla doesn't have her own fans. I follow both her and Taylor on Instagram and Twitter. Jayla is really funny and witty on Twitter. I wish I could be. I sort of lurk on social media a lot, but don't really post my own stuff. As a future famous author, I should probably be able to write something interesting in 140 characters or less.

Taylor glances over at us and says, "Hey, Nikki." I don't think she quite remembers my name. In fact, she shoots me a disdainful look and then turns back around, leaving only a swinging ponytail on my desk.

My fingers stretch out to touch the expensively streaked strands. I wonder if my hair could ever look that good. Nikki catches my eye and gives me a slight shake of her head. So I curl my chipped nails back into fists to help resist the temptation. It's probably a good thing, because I don't need Taylor Reed on my bad side. No one does.

Our high school, like most others, I suppose, has its groups. There's the jock crowd; the theater kids; the cowboys, surfers, and skaters; the smart kids; the Lovelies (and the boys who come and go around them); and then a leftover assortment of the rest. I am a leftover. Nikki, though, manages to exist among many groups, dipping in and out of the popular kids with ease.

Taylor reaches back and pulls her hair over her shoulder and out of my reach. It was probably getting dirty just by being on my desk.

I look toward Heather at the front of the room, hoping this meeting is going to get started on time. Now she's writing something on the board about the color scheme. Taylor, who has no concept of anyone else being the center of attention, talks and talks and talks to Jayla and Max. She's saying how she wants to go to the prom with the one person who really matters—her boyfriend, Liam Richardson. She wants it to be one of those nights that when she's thirty and someone asks her, "Who did you go to your prom with?" she's going to remember it perfectly. Because that's exactly what it will be. Perfect. The problem is, he hasn't actually asked her. Yet.

"I wish he would just *ask* me," she whines.

"I don't think you have to wait on some guy to ask you," Max drawls. "Just go."

"Without a date?" Taylor looks at him like he just grew three heads.

"With a date. Without a date. With a bunch of people. Who cares? It's one night."

I want to agree with Max. I *do* agree with Max. But I can't help but think that it *would* be nice to go to prom with someone special. I may not have a boyfriend, but I can imagine what it would be like—swept into a room filled with twinkling lights and chiffon dresses. Dancing. Flirting. Smiling. Kissing. It's a story just waiting to be written.

"Going with a group is out of the question," Taylor snaps. "I don't want to be part of a *crowd* at the most important event of my high school life." She shudders, then looks at Nikki. "Right?"

Nikki has been busy texting Jake, but she glances up and nods. "Yeah. Prom should be all about romance."

Jake hasn't asked Nikki to prom yet, but I know she's waiting.

I sigh.

Max leans over toward Jayla. "I like your nails," he says.

Jayla scoots her desk away, laughing. She has this great laugh that is way louder and bigger than anyone expects. Max scoots his desk closer to her.

"Don't touch them. You'll mess them up." She slaps his hand playfully, then turns away from him.

I wonder if all this flirting is leading somewhere. Maybe Max is rethinking his opinion on prom dates. But he's got to know Jayla is way out of his league. The rumor is she already has a date to prom with a senior basketball player named Derek Russell, who is six inches taller than Max.

Heather is trying to get everyone's attention again. "Hello? We need to get started."

No one even looks her way, and I feel a little sorry for her. Heather has this nervous thing she does where she blinks really fast. No one is sure if she is going to cry or if she has something in her eye or what, but lately Taylor and her friends have started doing it back to her and that just makes it worse.

"Can I have your attention?" Heather's voice gets louder and her right eye starts to twitch. If Taylor ever looks up from her phone, she's bound to notice. Mr. Landmann looks up from his reading and peers at Heather over his glasses, but he doesn't interrupt. Supervising after-school activities is all about empowering the student voice. Unless a fight breaks out or someone ugly-cries, he's not going to intervene.

Max decides to step up, more for the attention than out of kindness. "I think Heather needs everyone to listen."

The conversations stop, and all eyes turn toward Heather.

"Girls," she announces, then pauses and looks at Max, her right eye blinking rapidly. "And boy."

Max smiles at her and leans back in the desk like he is the boss of the world. A couple of girls give an obligatory giggle, and I know that only encourages him. Not surprisingly, Heather is one of the gigglers. I do a mental eye roll.

"Time to get down to business," Heather continues. "This year's junior-senior prom is going to be the best Huntsville High School has ever experienced, and it's all because of you."

She pauses like she expects applause, but there is no response. "Okay, this won't take long. Let's hear from our committee chairs. Facilities?"

Jayla speaks up. "Everything is set. We have security and the custodial staff scheduled for the whole night."

We all know the "staff" is really just one person. Mr. Thomas is the school custodian who occasionally puts on a name tag that reads "Security" for special events.

Heather nods. "Music?"

"I booked a local band called The Barneys," Max says. "They play a mix of stuff. I think it'll make everyone happy."

The classroom gives enthusiastic oohs and aahs. I've heard of The Barneys. I'm impressed. Heather continues with the roll call, and the responses pop up all over the room.

"Caterers?"

"Check."

"Photographer?"

"Check."

"Videographer?"

"Check."

"Decorations?"

There is a pause.

"Decorations? Nikki, wasn't that you?"

"Yes, but I need a clarification. Are we going to have a theme or not?" Nikki asks.

"I thought it was Enchanted Evening?" I ask, trying to help Nikki out and get this meeting moving along. I'm worried I'm going to be late to the library.

Taylor turns around to stare at me. Behind Taylor's shoulder, I see Heather take a few breaths to calm herself down. Her eyelids are still fluttering like some kind of ceiling fan, but their pace is slowing. Taylor narrows her ice-blue eyes at me.

"We don't want the same old thing," Heather explains. "It has to be unique."

Taylor nods enthusiastically. "Exactly. Even if the theme is familiar, you have to do something new with it."

"So Enchanted Evening or not?" Nikki asks.

"Yes," Heather says, "but edgy."

I'm not sure how edgy an enchanted evening can be, but Nikki nods like she totally gets it.

"So the color scheme?" Heather prompts. "Purple and black?"

"I vote for silver and gold," Nikki says. "The more sparkle, the better."

Heather looks around for confirmation, but no one seems to feel passionately about it one way or another.

Taylor finally says, "Okay with me. Glitter is my favorite color."

"So we have a theme and a color scheme. Decorations are able to move full speed ahead," Heather announces proudly. "Now, we just need someone to be in charge of social media. I've posted a few things on the Hornet, but we need way more than that." She glances around the room. "I'm looking for someone to spice things up and get some real buzz going."

Everyone looks at Torrey Grey, who is sitting three rows up and has been quiet the whole meeting. Torrey used to have a super-popular fashion vlog before she moved to our school last fall. She was kind of famous.

"Sorry, guys. Can't do it." Torrey holds up her hands. "I'm taking a break from social media."

No one else speaks up.

Nikki leans over and says to me, "I think you should do it."

Startled, I look up at her and shake my head no.

Absolutely not. No way. No how.

"You want to be a writer and this is writing stuff," Nikki whispers. "Online."

"That's not my kind of writing," I say. But then, in spite of myself, I start to think about it. I do have some ideas. I could post some videos of kids talking about prom. Maybe some Q&As. I could link to some prom fashion YouTube videos. My weird need to plan kicks in with a major jolt.

Maybe a little social media buzz might be good for *me*, too. Maybe I don't need to always be in Nikki's shadow.

When I was a kid, I took a pottery class. We made vases and bowls out of wet, heavy clay, then put them in a giant oven to harden. When they came out, I didn't want anyone to see my creation—a lopsided coffee cup with a wonky handle. It wasn't that I was scared of people making fun of it. Everyone's was a little off. But it was because it wasn't good enough and there was nothing I could do to make it better. It was done. Hard. Finished. When I brought it home, I threw it into the trash can and it shattered into pieces. High school may not be a piece of pottery, but it isn't finished yet. I still have a chance to make it better.

"I nominate Linden Wilson," Nikki says loudly.

This gets even Taylor's attention. She stares at Nikki, phone in hand, likes she's just waking up from a power nap. "You're kidding, right? Prom is the high school version of New York Fashion Week. It's a lot of pressure. We can't have just anyone in charge of publicity."

Gee, thanks, Taylor.

"Linden's going to be a famous writer one day. She'll be great at managing all the social media posts," Nikki says in her nobody's-going-to-argue-with-me voice.

Jayla speaks up, with the commanding voice that has served her well as volleyball team captain three years running. "I second the nomination for Linden Wilson to be our publicity chair."

I figure she's supporting me just to annoy Taylor, but I'll take it. Taylor looks back down at her phone and frowns, tapping away. "I don't even think I follow her on Instagram."

"I am on there," I say, a little sharply.

"Anyone opposed to Linden Wilson becoming our prom publicity chair?" Heather asks. I hold my breath, but no one says anything. Heather walks to the board, picks up a marker, and writes my name in block letters under the title of publicity director. I like the way it looks. So official. Maybe sharing my words with the public will be good practice for me, if I do want to become a real author one day. And maybe writing about the prom will inspire me.

I glance over to catch Nikki grinning at me because she was right and eventually I'm going to have to admit it. Coming to this meeting was a good idea.

"I accept the nomination," I say. Then I glance down at my phone. A pop-up message on Instagram informs me that Taylor Reed and Jayla Williams just followed me.

Welcome, new readers, I think. And I smile down at my cowboy boots.

CHAPTER TWO

The library is the only place where I don't have to try to fit in. It's effortless. Not like school, where everything is about trying harder and being better.

Here, people see me in a different way. Mr. Hooper, a well-dressed elderly man who is usually at the library looking for fashion magazines like *Vogue* and *Marie Claire*, refers to me as Texas's Next Top Model, which I think is hilarious. Maria Lucero, a friendly mom who mostly checks out early readers for her six-year-old twins, once pointed me out to another visitor as the short girl in the skinny jeans and cute shoes. And Mrs. Worthingham, who is usually looking for a book on goats, because she shows prizewinning goats at the Walker County Fair every year, once described me as "the fashionista at the fiction desk." But she spends a lot of time with goats, so I don't think she's much of an expert on style.

Here, in the library, I am confident and capable. Nobody knows about the average Linden from school.

Today, I sit cross-legged on the carpet in between the

shelves of books, with a mostly empty cart in the aisle beside me. I hear my coworker, Kat Lee, over in the story corner, reading a *Pat the Bunny* board book to a group of children. Even though I can't see them, I know they are sitting spellbound as Kat turns the pages and holds them up for everyone to see.

I've known Kat since elementary school, but somewhere in middle school we went different ways and to different crowds. Last year, when Nikki and I hit high school, I landed solidly in the middle tier of the popularity rankings—never hitting the top rung of the elite, but not sinking into the abyss of the unwashed either. Kat is somewhere out in the stratosphere of "I don't care what anyone thinks about me," which I greatly admire and secretly wish I could someday learn how to accomplish.

My journal lies blank at my side. I think of the Marty Speer Literary Prize. The deadline for the scholarship is only a few weeks away. My ticket to a summer in Austin, completely surrounded by all things writing, is rhythmically ticking down in my head . . . *Tick. Tick. Tick.*

I just need to write something to submit. But I haven't even started anything yet.

I stretch my arms out to their full length and wiggle all my fingers. Ready. I pick up my favorite black pen and the journal off the carpet.

Let's do this thing. Words, don't fail me now.

I wait.

The pen doesn't move. I usually write on my laptop, but I thought switching to my journal today would help the story ideas come faster.

It doesn't.

I lean back against the bottom shelf of books, my legs straight out in front of me, the pointy toes of my red boots aiming toward the ceiling. I'm in the final row of fiction and there's never much traffic back here. I take in a deep breath of book smell for inspiration.

Heaven.

Still, nothing comes.

I stare down at my fingers, willing them to start writing, but they just hover over the blank page, frozen and uninspired.

Is there another word for "uninspired"? I should look it up on my thesaurus—my favorite app on my phone. I firmly believe it is never good to be boxed in by only one word when there are so many to choose from. My thesaurus gives me options. Choices. Selections. Preferences. Alternatives. And even though the thesaurus says those words all mean the same thing, they definitely do not.

Each word has its own feel. *Murky* is not the same as *dim*.

I tap my pen against the page. Not too long ago, stories just poured out onto the page. I'd write and write, staying up all night or writing through the whole weekend. And when the stories were finished, I sometimes thought they were pretty good.

Just not good enough to share with anyone.

And that is the biggest problem with my writing—I don't want anyone to read it.

So how on earth am I going to enter this contest?

My phone buzzes. I look around. It buzzes again, and I pull it out of my back pocket.

NIKKI: CONGRATS, PUBLICITY DIRECTOR! ☺

I roll my eyes, look around to make sure no one is watching, then text back.

ME: CAN'T TALK NOW. WORKING.

NIKKI: COME OVER AFTER WORK. WE CAN MAKE A PLAN.

NIKKI: I HAVE CHOCOLATE!!

I can't help but smile when I read it. Nikki knows me well. She knows I don't believe in saving chocolate for the blues. Chocolate is for celebration. Before I can answer, I hear footsteps. I'm caught. Mrs. Longshore, the librarian, hates when we use our phones at work. Shoving the phone into my pocket, I stumble to my feet, kicking my journal underneath the shelf of books.

But it's not Mrs. Longshore walking toward me. Instead, it's a guy from school, Alex Rivera. I know who Alex is because everyone pretty much knows everyone at Huntsville High School, even if they don't hang out together. Besides, Alex used to take jujitsu classes with my older brother.

"Can I help you?" I ask as he gets closer. He is looking at me and not the books.

"Do you work here?" Alex asks.

I nod.

"I'm Linden Wilson," I say, even though he probably knows who I am, too. "And since you're going to ask sooner or later, I'm not a genius like my brother. Sorry."

Alex looks confused. "Who?"

"Theodore Wilson," I say. "He's my brother."

He still looked confused, so I say, "Rat."

My brother has an unusual, but memorable, nickname. His senior picture was just on the front page of the *Huntsville Item* last week because he got accepted to all eight Ivy League schools. So it's no secret that he's seriously brilliant.

"Ohhhhh." Alex smiles when he finally makes the connection. "Yeah, Rat *is* kind of a genius." Then he pauses, raising his eyebrows at me. "But . . . you're not?"

I shake my head. "I'm not a lot of things," I say. *I'm not beautiful like Taylor. I'm not confident like Nikki. I'm not strong like my mother.* "So, I try harder. Sorry."

It's a joke, but not really. Why am I suddenly opening up to this random guy?

"You shouldn't apologize for what you're not," he says, pulling a copy of Paul Zindel's *The Pigman* off the shelf and flipping through a few pages. When he looks up from the book, he meets my gaze. "So, if you're not a genius like your brother, what are you?"

The question takes me by surprise.

What am I?

"Can I get back to you on that?" I ask.

He nods, smiling, and then asks, "Do you guys carry audiobooks?"

Ah. A normal question. I'm relieved for a minute, but then I stop, "Wait. You don't get off that easily. What are *you*?"

He doesn't think about that for very long. "I'm a good baseball player . . . And, ummm . . . " He snaps his fingers. "Thanks to years of braces, I have *very* straight teeth."

He gives me an over-exaggerated smile and I can confirm this fact.

"And I'm a pretty good big brother, even though my little sister has gotten me in trouble more times than I can count." He laughs. "I was grounded once for a month when I cut her ponytail off. She was six at the time."

"How old is she now?"

"She'll be fifteen in a couple of weeks," he says, sliding the book back into the waiting space and turning to face me.

"I sympathize with your sister. Brothers can be a real pain."

Alex shrugs. "So. Was that answer good enough to get me an escorted trip to the audiobooks?"

"Absolutely." I retrieve my journal from under the shelf. Alex notices, and gives me a quizzical smile. I try not to blush. Then I lead the way back toward the audiobooks.

"See, my baseball coach recommended I start running to get in shape for spring baseball season," Alex explains, falling into step beside me. "But I don't really like running."

"Neither do I," I say. "Unless I'm running *from* something."

Alex laughs. I remember then that he's part of the jock crowd. I'm not sure why he's chatting me up, but I could definitely get used to it.

"I tried listening to music, and that helped," Alex goes on as we round the corner. "But I was falling behind on schoolwork. So I was sitting in English yesterday and had this great idea. I don't have to read *To Kill a Mockingbird*. I can listen to it," he tells me. "While I run."

"That is a good idea," I admit.

I feel someone watching us and my eyes shift. Kat is standing at the circulation desk across the room. She smirks at me and gives me a thumbs-up behind Alex's back. Instantly, heat inches up my throat, but I act like I don't see her.

"All the audiobooks are up by the magazine racks," I tell Alex, then pull a copy of *To Kill a Mockingbird* off the shelf. "Here you go."

He looks down at it in my hand and then, out of nowhere, he says, "I like your boots."

"Thanks," I say, surprised he noticed.

"I have a confession to make." His ears are turning bright red.

I'm almost afraid to ask. "What?"

He clears his throat. "I know who you are," he says. "And I didn't come to the library *just* for the audiobooks."

I'm not sure I understand where he's going with this, but then he says, "I wanted to talk to you."

"To me?" I'm stunned. What does he mean?

Slowly, he says, "I asked Rat where you worked."

"You don't need the book?"

"Well, I do. I want to listen to the book, but I thought maybe . . ." Alex stops and swallows hard. "I could see you, too."

I must look as shocked as I feel. Alex . . . . wanted to see *me*? I'd never even thought he knew who I was. We don't exactly run in the same circles.

The truth is, I've been sneaking looks at Alex ever since he applied a joint lock to defeat my brother in a jujitsu match last summer. But now I see all of him for the first time. Really see him. He is compact. Not much taller than me, but solid. Thick black hair. Warm brown, almost black, eyes. Brown, smooth skin. It is like he suddenly materializes out of a boy I thought I knew.

I let out a nervous laugh. The best-kept secret in all of Huntsville High School is looking back at me, and something just clicks into place inside my brain. I'm not sure what I'm supposed to say, but he's standing there staring at me with those dark brown eyes and his ears are all bright pink, so I say, "That's nice."

Stupid. Stupid. Stupid!

Alex shifts from one foot to the other, jams his hands into the pockets of his jeans, and his ears get even redder. "I was wondering if you ever go to the baseball games?" Alex asks.

"No," I say, but I don't want to discourage him, so I add, "but I've always wanted to."

Then Alex says, "How about I buy you a snow cone after my baseball game tomorrow?"

"Sure," I say. "I like big spenders." Then I worry he thinks I'm serious, so I add, "Just kidding," but he's already laughing.

"So, I'll see you tomorrow?" he asks, taking the audiobook out of my hand.

I nod.

Did Alex Rivera just ask me out?

Oh. My. God.

Something amazing just happened. To me!

"He's cute," Kat says, joining me at the desk after Alex leaves. Her sleeveless red dress shows off amazing biceps, toned to perfection by hours of mixed martial arts. The tattoo on her inner arm says "Darcy" in a bold, black scroll and is today's reminder of her devotion to all things Jane Austen. Tomorrow, it will probably say something different because all of Kat's tattoos are temporary and wash off with soap and water. She says she has a hard time with commitment.

I mentally kick myself for underestimating her. Of course she noticed. Even so, I still try to act like I don't have a clue. "Who?"

"Like you don't know." Kat laughs. "I know sparks when I see them."

Me and Alex Rivera? Sparks?

"You don't know anything," I mumble under my breath, and she glares at me.

I give up. "Was it that obvious?"

"Only to me and everyone else who saw you two googly-eyeing each other." Kat logs in to the computer station.

This is a problem. I didn't need Kat tainting this . . . thing with Alex. Whatever it is.

"We're just friends," I say, because that's what everybody says when they don't know what else to say. But are Alex and I even friends? What are we to each other now? My head is still spinning from our interaction. From the talk of audiobooks and running and snow cones . . .

Surprisingly, Kat drops the interrogation—for now.

"Why were you late today, anyway?" she asks me. "Detention?" Then she laughs at the absurdity of her question because she knows I've never been to detention.

I glance over at her, and brace myself for her sneer. "I was at the prom planning meeting. I was elected publicity chair."

Her lips twitch into a smile. "Congratulations," she says solemnly.

"You think it's silly," I say, sliding my hands under the stack of books and standing up carefully. I put a couple more on top, stacking all the books up into one extra-tall column, and move them over to the cart behind the desk.

"I'm not saying it's silly. It's fine if you want to go to prom," Kat says. "It's just not my thing."

"I don't know if I'm going," I say. "I'm just helping."

"What do you have to do as 'publicity chair'?" She makes air quotes.

"I have to write some posts on the Hornet . . . "

"The Hornet? Really?" She smirks.

"It's just the starting point," I assure her.

"Let me see," she says, scooting out of the way and waving me toward the computer.

I roll my chair over and pull up the Hornet. There's Heather's old post about the prom from earlier today.

"You do have your work cut out for you," Kat says, scrolling down the page. Then she stops, squinting at something on-screen. "Hey. What's this Worthy thing?"

"Oh, yeah." I'd forgotten about the app. Checking to make sure Mrs. Longshore isn't around, I take my phone out of my pocket. Then I tap the Worthy icon and it opens. "It's this new app," I say, showing it to Kat.

Welcome to Worthy! the screen reads. *A private network for Huntsville High School students to share honest opinions about the weaknesses and strengths of select couples. Swipe here to continue.*

"Huh?" Kat says. " 'Select couples'? Who's doing the selecting?"

"I don't know," I say, feeling kind of nervous. But I obey the app and swipe to get to the next screen.

There, in the middle of the screen, is a photo of Taylor Reed and her boyfriend, Liam Richardson. It's clearly been lifted from Taylor's Instagram. She and Liam are standing on the football field, Liam all sweaty and handsome in his uniform after a game. His arms are around Taylor's waist and she's making a kissy face at the camera. Their names are written out above the photo.

And underneath the photo, in big block letters, is one question:

IS SHE WORTHY?

There are two answers to choose from. Yes, with a little heart, or no, with a big red *X*. I am intrigued in spite of myself. My finger hovers over the heart.

"What *is* this?" Kat asks, shifting closer to me.

"I'm not sure. Like a popularity contest for a couple? You vote on whether they make a good match or not?"

Taylor and Liam are obviously a good match. They're the super couple of Huntsville High School. They've plastered all of social media with photos of themselves looking gorgeous together. Like the picture that's on Worthy: celebrating at the football game (#firstfootballwin). Walking through the fall leaves (#fallfunwithbae). Lying out by the pool (#hotdate). Even feeding each other Tater Tots in the cafeteria (#yummy).

"Who started the app?" Kat asks.

"Don't know," I answer. "But it probably wouldn't be that complicated to make."

"Obviously," Kat says. "Anyone who's taken Tech I would know how to create this piece of bland. I could do it in my sleep."

"So what do you think?" I ask, looking at the picture of Taylor and Liam. "*Is* she worthy?"

"Why is this only about the girl?" Kat asks. "Why does she have to be worthy of *him*?"

"Good question," I say. "One you should be asking every fashion magazine article ever written. But I figure this is no different than liking someone's photo on Facebook or Instagram, right?"

Kat frowns.

I notice that, if I scroll down on the app, there are comments posted. Some are pretty harsh.

Eww, she's evil.

She's not worthy of anyone!

Not surprisingly, Taylor has made some enemies over the years. And behind fake screen names, everyone's snarky side is coming out in full force. I guess it makes it easier for people to be rude if they don't have to face the person they are talking about in real life.

And other comments are obviously written by Taylor's BFFs.

Of course she's worthy. She's hot. Everyone who disagrees is just really jealous.

"Are they going to show the results?" Kat asks. "It seems kind of gross."

I shrug. "But it's probably just part of being in the popular crowd. Everyone has an opinion about you. They're used to it."

Kat stands up. "I'm out," she says, turning away to pull a bunch of DVDs out of the return box.

"Well, I think they seem perfect for each other," I say, with a slight sneer. I push the Yes button underneath the picture. "Mr. and Mrs. Perfect."

My finger hovers over the keypad. Should I write a comment?

No, I decide. I won't let myself get sucked in entirely. Just voting is enough.

Taylor Reed & Liam Richardson

IS SHE WORTHY?

Here's what you are saying:

* Eww, she's evil.

* She's not worthy of anyone!

* Has anyone ever seen these two apart? Don't they ever get bored of each other? I would!

* Of course Taylor is totally worthy of him. The only thing they fight about is blocking each other's view of the mirror.

* She couldn't survive without him. He's the perfect accessory.

* Have you ever noticed that one of her eyebrows is higher than the other?

✻ Why is everyone slamming her???? She's gorgeous and you all know it.

✻ Of course she's worthy. She's hot. Everyone who disagrees is just really jealous.

✻ SMH. Seriously, you guys will vote for pretty instead of smart and talented every day.

✻ Perfection isn't real.

✻ TBH, I've never thought she was that hot. He could do better.

✻ Taylor Reed is pretty enough on the outside! Too bad she's so shallow and stupid.

Comments now closed. Voting is complete! Stay tuned for the result . . .

CHAPTER THREE

"You were supposed to be here thirty minutes ago," Nikki says when she opens the front door.

I frown. "Hello to you, too."

Nikki steps aside and lets me into her house.

"Hey, Mrs. Aquino." I wave to Nikki's mom on the way through the kitchen.

"You want to stay for dinner, Linden?" Mrs. Aquino calls back. "We're having adobo and pancit."

Mrs. Aquino knows how much I love her cooking, especially when she makes Filipino food. She also knows my mom is not the best cook in the world.

"Can't tonight, Mrs. Aquino," I say with a sigh. "Thanks."

The Aquino house is always full of people and noise. So different from my empty, quiet house. That's why I love hanging out here. Tonight, Nikki's older sister, Perla, is sitting at the kitchen table doing homework. Just like every night for the last two weeks, Perla is arguing with her mother. According to Nikki, all Perla cares about right now is leaving Huntsville, Texas, and going away to college. The problem is that the Aquinos can't afford the college Perla wants to attend. So every evening turns into a battle-ground between Perla and her mother. Nikki says she just tries to ignore them both, but it never works.

Mrs. Aquino's voice is tense. "If you live at home for a year, we can make it work the next year. I promise."

"Do you know how hard it is to get into Brown?" Perla isn't yelling, but her voice is angry. "It's one of the top schools in the country."

"Yes, Perla. It's an amazing accomplishment. I know how hard you worked for it, but we just can't afford fifty thousand dollars in tuition right now," Mrs. Aquino says.

"I made the grades to be accepted to a real university. Not some community college." Now Perla is yelling.

"It doesn't have to be a community college. You can go to Sam Houston State. Just stay for one year. That's all I'm asking."

The desperation on Mrs. Aquino's face makes me want to fix it somehow, but there is nothing I can do except follow Nikki out of the kitchen.

"Hi, Linden." Maricel, Nikki's little sister, waves at me from the couch, then goes back to watching *The Walking Dead*. Maricel is really into zombies, and she has the show turned up loud enough to drown out the arguing in the kitchen.

"Scary," I say to Maricel. She nods, but doesn't look away from the television.

"She's already told me she wants to be a zombie for Halloween," Nikki says on the way upstairs to her room.

"It's March," I say.

"She likes Halloween *and* zombies."

"What does she think about Jake?" I ask. Maricel might only be ten, but she's a good judge of character.

"Don't know."

"He hasn't been over?"

"Not yet," Nikki says. "Maricel is sometimes a goofball with new people."

I wonder if the issue is with Maricel or with Jake, but it's not worth the argument. I follow Nikki down the hall and into her room.

As always, the green wall of Nikki's small bedroom is covered in masking-taped-notes and chart-paper sheets and sticky pads. Magic marker arrows connect fabric and photos to drawings in some kind of elaborate spider web that only Nikki understands. Large red question marks pepper the chart at various locations, and smaller yellow sticky notes are randomly sprinkled throughout the whole jumble with carefully printed questions on each, like, "What color?" and "What if?" The mannequin beside Nikki's desk is named Sally. Instead of a punching bag to pound away stupid people's perceptions of fat girls in a skinny world, Nikki has Sally. But instead of hitting her, Nikki pins pieces of fabric and bits of material from clothes she carefully rips apart and reconstructs. She says it's her way of working out her anger and frustration. Nikki always tells me Sally wants to come alive and walk outside in the sunshine. Those scraps of fabric and paper want to swirl around her knees in yellows and blues. They want texture and substance. Eventually they will become a Nikki Aquino Creation, just like the skirt I am wearing today.

I throw my backpack on the floor of Nikki's bedroom and flop across her Laura Ashley comforter.

"I can tell you have something to say, so spill it." Nikki flips through a magazine at her desk, a pile of books and homework untouched on the floor beside her chair.

"Like what?" I try to make my voice all innocent, but it doesn't work. I can't hold it in any longer.

Nikki squints at me. "Is it a chocolate kind of day?"

"I'm not sure. Do you know Alex Rivera?" I ask.

"Sure. The baseball player, right? Kind of quiet." Nikki tears out a picture of a blue flowered teacup from the magazine, then stands to tack it onto Sally the mannequin. The image joins other scraps and pieces of creations-to-be. Pale pink satin. Ivory lace. Peach tulle. Bright red ribbons. Buttery-smooth leather. Robin's-egg-blue silk. I know that little square of torn paper will someday be transformed into something amazing. "Why?" She sits back down and faces me, looking intrigued.

"He came into the library today and . . . " I stop for dramatic effect. I can feel myself blushing.

"And?"

"I think, um . . . I think he asked me out."

"*Shut up!* Really?" Nikki leans forward in her chair, letting the magazine slip to the floor. "Oh my God, Linden! What did he say?"

"Well, he asked me to come to his baseball game on Thursday, and then he said . . ."

"Who said what?" Maricel is standing at the open door with a plate of lumpia in her hands.

"You're supposed to knock," Nikki says.

"Mom sent up a snack." Maricel comes in without an invitation, hands the plate to Nikki, and makes herself at home on the carpet in front of the bed. "So who said what?" she repeats, looking at me with a conspiratorial smile.

"None of your business, Nosy Pants." Nikki resorts to name-calling like she's Maricel's age, but Nosy Pants doesn't seem to mind. She just keeps chattering away, forgetting her original question for now.

"Next month I'm going to be eleven," she says to me, "and you know what that means, right?"

"Not really," I answer automatically. Nothing is going to get this kid to leave us alone.

"Come on." Nikki's grabs her hand and pulls her to her feet.

Maricel pulls away from Nikki's grasp and leans in toward me on her tiptoes. "It means I get to go to middle school next year, and . . . you know what that means, don't you?"

"I guess not," I say.

Maricel is enjoying the guessing game. Nikki is not. She stands up and walks over to the door, holding it open. "Get out, Mari. We're talking about private stuff."

But Maricel is determined to tell me. "It means boys are going to be asking me out, too."

"Out," Nikki yells, pointing toward the hall.

With a final twirl, Maricel turns and walks out the door. Nikki closes it firmly behind her.

"Finally." Nikki collapses back into her desk chair. "Now tell me all about it."

I laugh. "It seemed so not real. He said he'd buy me a snow cone after the game. I think . . . I *think* that's a date, right?"

"It so is!" Nikki exclaims. "Boys don't just ask girls to baseball games out of nowhere, you know." She sits down on the bed beside me. "This is really exciting, Linden. Do you like him?"

My heart races. "I don't even know him that well . . . but he's cute." *Really cute*, I think, remembering his big dark eyes.

Nikki is grinning. "Do you think he'll ask you to prom?"

I let out a laugh. "Prom? Nikki, we just talked today for the first time ever. I'm not even sure we're going on a real date! How can I think about prom already?"

Nikki frowns. "How could you not? Maybe I could say something to Alex . . . drop a hint . . . "

My shoulders tense. "Don't get involved, Nikki."

"Are you sure?" she asks.

I sit up straight. "*Yes.*"

"Okay. I won't." Nikki holds out her hands to stop me from freaking out. "Not now, anyway."

"Not ever," I say. I feel a muscle in my neck start to twitch. "This isn't about you."

"Okay," she says. Then she adds, "Now, speaking of prom, I have something to tell *you*."

"What is it?" I ask, even though I can already guess.

"Jake asked me!" Nikki squeals and claps her hands. "When I got to the parking lot after school, he'd decorated my car with flowers and was standing there waiting for me. He said there was no one else he wanted to take to prom but me. Isn't that amazing?"

"Amazing," I echo. Promposals like that are all the rage now; people can't just ask each other, there has to be a whole event planned around the asking. "I'm happy for you," I say, and I mean it, but I'm also full of doubt.

Nikki is quiet. "Can't you just give Jake a chance?" she asks. She looks down at her feet so I can't see her eyes. "He thinks you don't like him."

"I like him." My voice comes out flat and sarcastic. We both know I'm lying. I wish I could pretend to like the people I don't, but my face gives it all away. Nikki hates that about me. But then there's the way Jake doesn't even look at me most of the time. Like I don't even exist. Like I'm part of the wall or the floor. Nikki would never understand that feeling. She's never been invisible in her whole life. I take a deep breath. I have to be careful or whatever I say next will be wrong. It always is where Jake was concerned.

"Do *you* like him?" I ask.

"You know I do," Nikki whispers. "I . . . I think I love him."

"Then what does it matter what I think about him?" I blurt it out, brusque and loud. Instantly, her face closes off.

"It matters." She leans forward, her hands clenched into fists. "I wish it didn't, but it does."

I take another deep breath. "Look, I'm sorry."

My apology is sincere, but we both know I will not change my mind about Jake. Nikki stands and walks back to her desk. She picks up the sharpened blue charcoal pencil off the desktop in front of her and writes a word on the top yellow sticky note.

Ruching?

She peels the bright yellow square off the top of the stack and then carefully places it on the wall beside two notes that read *Roses?* and *Lace?*

"How is the dress coming along?" I ask, trying to fill up the awkward silence. Nikki has been working on her prom dress for over a week now. She can't wait to walk into our gym wearing a Nikki Aquino Creation

"I've narrowed it down to two possibilities." Nikki turns to the computer on her desk and pulls up a picture, rolling her chair out of the way so I can see. "I'm thinking something like this."

"Cool. I like the mermaid silhouette," I say, glad things feel back to normal again. "That's new, right?"

"You like it better than the ballroom style?"

"Definitely. It will show off your curves perfectly."

She nods slowly, contemplating the photo. "I hope Jake likes it."

My heart sinks a little bit. Shouldn't that be beside the point? Everyone will like it. No one else in the room will be wearing a dress as fabulous as Nikki's.

Nikki's gaze suddenly shifts to look at me, and her eyes narrow. Uh-oh. I know that look.

"You should have worn a green shirt with that skirt. Lime green with a lot of yellow undertones. Like the stems and leaves of the tulips." I can tell by the faraway look in her eyes she is picturing it. "The white is all wrong."

"I don't have a green shirt," I say.

"It's a problem."

"Nobody wears green shirts," I say, and then watch as she walks over to her closet and picks out a green T-shirt to wave in my face. I should have known.

"I don't think shirts are what I need to be focused on right now." I sigh loudly and pick at the pillow in my lap. "I should never have volunteered to be in charge of prom publicity. What was I thinking?"

"Are you kidding? It's the perfect job for you. Everyone will be amazed at how creative you are," Nikki insists. "You're going to blow them away."

I hope she's right. "Nobody in my family has a creative bone in their body. My dad is all about biology and nature. All my mom wants to do is save lives . . . "

"That's pretty important."

"And then, of course, there's Rat. He's in a category all his own. They're all so . . . " I pause. "Practical."

"And that's exactly why you need to jump in and do something totally different that will make a name for yourself. Something that is *you*."

"I was thinking . . . " I sit up on the side of the bed. "I could film some promposals and put them up on the page. Maybe ask for a heads-up when it's going to happen so I can be there to film it?"

Nikki nods. "Immortalize it." She pauses, and adds, "Too bad you weren't there when Jake asked."

"Yeah," I say, and then I feel the awkwardness between us again.

I reach into my book bag and take out my laptop. I open it, power up, and type down a couple of notes about promposals. Energy snaps through my brain. The ideas are starting to flow.

"What about putting up prom fashion tips on the Hornet?" I wonder out loud. "I could interview Torrey Grey? And you could do a makeup tutorial?"

"Ooh, I like it," Nikki says. "See, I told you you'd be good at this."

A thought takes hold. If I do it right, this publicity thing could be my ticket to making me better than average. It's a chance to tip the scales and put me on the plus side of popularity.

Nikki motions to the plate sitting on her nightstand. "Do you want a lumpia?"

I raise my eyebrows. "Why don't you want it?"

"I need to stay away from carbs. With my build, even a few pounds can be noticeable."

"Jake said that?" I ask. Another reason not to like Jake. Like I need any more.

"Of course not," Nikki says, but I'm not sure if I believe her. All of sudden I want to hug her and whisper in her ear, "Don't listen to Jake Edwards." But she isn't going to hear me.

"So, I guess you can watch me eat." I pick up the Filipino egg roll and take a huge bite. "Ummmmm."

She doesn't seem tempted and it worries me. I take another bite and chew slowly. Nikki might never be a size two, but that's never stopped her from wearing what she wanted to wear. No way was she going to wear some dress from the women's section that looked like some kind of tablecloth that would attract bees.

It started a few years ago, with a two-dollar skirt from Goodwill that she tore apart, seam by seam. Then she reconstructed it on an old sewing machine she bought at a yard sale, studying what happened when she changed a bit here and took up a bit there. The result was that she needed to get another skirt and start the process all over again. So she did. Again. And again.

Just like I rewrite my stories over and over to make them better, Nikki perfected her designs with excruciating attention to detail. Our final creations were very different, but we inspired each other. I would tell Nikki a story about a girl who needed the perfect skirt to wear to a picnic in Central Park. And in return, my main character would wear that skirt, in all of its Nikki Aquino glory, on the pages of my story.

Even though I never let anyone read the stories. Not even Nikki.

But Nikki wasn't so shy about sharing. Eventually, all the trial and error paid off, and now she wears her creations to school on a regular basis. At first, there were a few compliments here and there, but it was never about what other people thought. It was about Nikki and the way she wanted to look. Maybe that's why this whole thing with Jake Edwards is such a shock. Somehow he slipped under Nikki Aquino's skin, and I don't like it one bit.

I force a smile and change the subject. "So what should I wear to the game to see Alex?" I ask.

Nikki pulls out a sketch pad and starts to draw quickly. She slides the paper over to me. "I'd suggest some boyfriend jeans. Maybe with a tank top and a cardigan?"

I nod. "The white wrap one?"

She bites her lower lip and thinks about it a minute. "That could work. Do you want me to come over and do your makeup before I go to work?"

I nod gratefully. "I don't know what I'd do without you."

A smile spreads slowly across her face. "Without me you'd be wearing T-shirts with puppies on them everywhere," she says.

"But great shoes."

"True. I don't know how your shoe Spidey-sense some-how developed when every other fashion sense didn't . . . "

"I'm a shoe superhero," I say. And Nikki nudges me and laughs, and just like that, Jake Edwards and prom seem very far away.

CHAPTER FOUR

It's already dark by the time I leave Nikki's house. I'm exhausted, but my mind is still working on the publicity ideas. I wish I could come up with something that would make everyone sit up and take notice. I don't want to keep feeling like I'm always behind—with fingers grasping, arms reaching, stretching—but never getting there.

I shouldn't care what everybody thinks about me, but I do.

When I pull into the driveway, Max Rossi is sprawled out in a tangled mess of legs and skateboard on the sidewalk. It is always amazing to me how he can recover from fall after fall. It is even more amazing how he still thinks skateboarding is cool when he is obviously so bad at it.

Slowly he gets to his feet and picks up the skateboard.

I put my head down on the steering wheel and whisper, "No. No. No."

Not tonight, Max. Not in the mood.

When I lift my head, I see Max walk across the front yard toward the driveway, carrying the skateboard. He lifts one hand in greeting, and I know I can't ignore him no matter how bad I want to. I open the car door and get out.

Over the years, Max and I have cycled through almost every stage of friendship. When I was six, I built a tent out of tablecloths and he managed to destroy it with his remote-controlled helicopter. At age eleven, when Nikki and I designed a new line of fashionable headbands, he dropped water balloons on our runway show from the tree limb above. When we were twelve, we shared our first kiss in the tree house his dad built. Then we went to high school, made new friends, and went our different ways. Max grew out of his awkward stage and into the popular crowd. This year he was even elected junior class president. So now we don't talk much, even though he tries sometimes. Especially when it's just in the neighborhood and no one better is around.

"What's up?" he asks when I get out of the car.

"Not much." I feel sticky and my shirt clings to my back, making me want a shower. In a few more months, when the heat of the Texas summer builds to unbearable heights, I'll be taking showers twice a day.

"Did you see that thing about Taylor? The app?"

I nod. "Does anyone know who did it?"

"No, but it's spreading like crazy."

"Good for her," I say, and slam the car door shut behind me.

"So . . . what's this I hear about you and Alex?" He stumbles over his words awkwardly.

I pause, my backpack halfway to my shoulder. He definitely has my attention now. "Alex? What exactly are you hearing?"

"He was asking me about you the other day at baseball practice. I guess he knows we live near each other."

"And?" I wait, every muscle frozen until I hear his answer.

"I said you were great."

I let out a long breath. "Thanks, I guess." I pull my backpack up on one shoulder and start toward the house. I need to think about this new information. Alex is talking about me to other guys? Is that a good thing?

"So he likes you?" Max sounds doubtful. Like it couldn't possibly be true. Leave it to Max to ruin everything.

"You don't think I'm likable?" I ask him.

"You know I've always liked you, Linden. You have your own style. It's just a shame to think you're going to go out with someone like Alex."

I turn to face him. "What's wrong with Alex?"

"Nothing." Max snorts. "That's kind of the issue, don't you think?"

"What is that supposed to mean?" I stare at him.

He thinks for a second, then says, "He's not exactly your type. You deserve someone a little higher up on the popularity radar."

My throat tightens. When we were eight, Max dared me to jump off the high dive at the pool. Being a natural-born scaredy-cat, it's hard to believe I agreed. Adrenaline, and pure stubbornness, kicked in enough to get me up the stairs and out to the end of the board. But when I looked at that water shimmering so far below, and all that air in between, I just couldn't do it. Crippling panic slammed into the backs of my knees, leaving my legs quaking so badly the board under my feet started to sway. I turned around slowly, away from the edge, then dropped to my hands and knees to crawl back to safety. Everyone waiting to go next had to get off the ladder, sneering and giggling, so I could get back down again. The worst part of all was that Max didn't even say a thing. He just looked at me and shook his head in disappointment. Sort of like how he was looking at me right now.

"Whatever," I say, and keep walking toward the house. I fire one final shot back over my shoulder. "You're just jealous because I'm dating someone and you're not."

"Are you sure you're dating Alex? 'Cause I haven't seen any dates yet."

I stop, then turn to face him. "For your information, we're going out tomorrow."

"Funny. He didn't say anything about that to me." He glances over at a car passing down the street, then back at me.

"He doesn't have to tell you everything," I say.

"True." He shrugs. "I guess it's a good thing you're dating someone now that you're in charge of prom publicity."

I frown. "What do you mean?"

"Well, you're going to prom, right? You really have to go now that you're in charge of it. It'd be downright hypocritical not to . . . " His voice trails off and he grins his know-it-all grin, letting his words sink in. Then he adds, "Sort of like false advertisement."

A hot flush spreads over me. "Of course I'm going."

Max gives me one of his slimy little half smiles, like he doesn't believe me.

"Who are *you* taking to the prom?" I ask, even though I don't really care.

"I'm leaving my options open right now," he says. He runs one hand through his blond hair, brushing it back from his forehead. "Maybe I'll just go by myself. Less pressure."

"Yeah. Sure," I say, turning my back to him for the final time. I'm done with Max Rossi. But as usual, he doesn't seem to get the hint, because he just stands there and watches me with his skateboard in his hands, shifting from one foot to the other.

I hate that what he's said has gotten to me. *What if I don't have a date to prom?* I think as I climb the steps to my house. What if I end up not going at all? If I make a success of this publicity job, everyone will notice. I don't want to turn into some kind of pitiful joke. I can just hear Taylor Reed whispering to her friends now: "Poor thing did all this work and she didn't even get to go."

Then I think about the feel of a dress swishing against

my legs and the music playing in the background. Everything suddenly turns upside down in my head. I want to go to the prom, and I'm going to do everything possible to make it happen. I just need a plan.

A message dings across my phone from Worthy. I should have turned off the push notifications when I downloaded the app. Or maybe I shouldn't have downloaded it at all. I slide the phone out of sight into the outside pocket of my backpack and push open the front door.

Instantly I'm bombarded by a happy, wiggling Labrador retriever sliding across the hardwood floors and into my legs.

"Hi, Murphy." I lean down to pet the dog, wishing everyone was so happy to see me.

Murphy flops over onto his back at my feet and I give him a quick tummy rub.

The living room is dark, but the smell of baking cookies and a light are coming from the kitchen. I throw my backpack over on the couch.

"Hey, Linden. Come here, honey. I want to show you something," Mom calls out.

I go into the next room, Murphy bouncing along beside me.

My mom never made cookies, or anything else, from scratch until she became a firefighter. Then cooking turned into a competition just like everything else. Her first attempt was chocolate chip cookies. Every day, I'd come home to a different batch. We ate chocolate chip cookies for weeks, while she meticulously researched, and then perfected, the recipe. There were cookies with white chocolate chips, and chocolate chip cookies with three kinds of nuts—walnuts, pecans, and almonds. She even made chocolate chip cookies with marshmallows. Nobody in our family complained, but it was like a whole new Mom. In many ways.

Tonight, Mom is sitting at the table wearing a faded blue T-shirt and drinking a Dr Pepper out of a can. The cooking channel is playing on the television on the countertop, but for once she isn't watching.

"You're not going to believe this." She pushes something across the table. It's the Huntsville Firefighter Calendar. "Look at August."

I flip over the pages, then stop to stare at the photo. "Wow. Congratulations, Mom."

The picture for August is my mom wearing a black tank top, black pants, her bright yellow suspenders, and a bright yellow helmet. Behind her is one of the big ladder trucks, and she has a heavy yellow fire hose hoisted up on one shoulder. Her sculpted shoulders are impressive and her biceps are the result of hours of hard work that can't be seen in the photo.

"Great guns, Mom," I say. I lean forward with both elbows on the table to get a better look.

"I'm the only woman who made it." She smiles proudly. "This is just the draft; it won't go to print until late summer. Just in time for Christmas."

My mom used to be an elementary school teacher, but last year she called a family meeting and told us all that she always wanted to become a firefighter. Who knew? We certainly didn't. She tried out three times before she made it, training every day to get stronger and stronger. Now there always seems to be a fireman or two lounging around on couches or rummaging through the fridge. Firefighters work four days in a row with the next three days off, which makes for a strange family life sometimes. But my dad takes it all in stride. He is the mellowest person on the planet, which is good because he has to put up with a lot. Or at least I think he's putting up with it.

"You look amazing," I say. We both stare down at the picture for a few more minutes before Mom asks, "How did your day go?"

"Okay," I say, slipping down into a chair beside her. "I made a ninety-two on my math test."

Mom looks toward the television and picks up the pen in front of her to jot down a few notes on the legal pad lying beside the calendar. Alton Brown is making meat loaf.

They rotate cooking duties at the firehouse, and next Wednesday is her day to cook. She is determined to be the best cook at the firehouse when her turn comes up.

She watches the television, but says to me, "What did you gets points off for?"

I cross my arms over my chest and stare straight ahead. Never enough.

I stretch my legs out underneath the table and frown. "Stop."

"What?" Mom finally, actually looks at me.

"It's a good grade," I say.

"Of course it is." She looks mystified. "What did I say?"

She isn't even aware of what's she's doing. "Never mind." I straighten and stand up, heading toward the fridge. I can't do anything right these days where my mother is concerned.

Be an engineer. An architect. Create something important. Like a building.

She doesn't have to tell me everything I do isn't important. I know. I get tired of being in everyone's shadow. Especially when my own mother can't even see me lurking there.

"You have the grades to be anything you want," my mom mumbles behind me. It is an all-too-familiar conversation, and tonight I will not respond.

"I went to a meeting after school today to help plan the prom," I say. "They elected me publicity chair."

"Are you going to the prom?" she asks, surprised.

"Why wouldn't I?"

"You just haven't said anything about it until now," she says.

"Well, I'm going." That's two people I've said it to now. If I keep saying it out loud, it has to be true.

"Good for you," Mom says. I can tell she thinks it's

probably a complete waste of time and money. She doesn't ask any questions.

I change the subject. "Where's Rat?"

"He's at some chemistry club meeting," Mom says, frowning at the nickname. She refuses to call him anything but Theodore, but I gave in to Rat a long time ago. "I think he's having dinner with Ever. Can you fend for yourself?"

Ever is my brother's girlfriend. Even though Rat might not seem like the dressing-up kind of guy, he asked Ever to the prom weeks ago. My mom didn't act at all surprised, nor did she give him any lectures on not buying into the social norms. Maybe because he and Ever are seniors and have been dating for over a year. Or maybe because my brother is always doing something unexpected. It's normal for Rat to be unpredictable.

"Where are you going?" I ask my mom, getting the milk out of the fridge. Evidently, it is going to be a Cheerios kind of night.

Mom jots some notes down on the paper in front of her about Alton Brown's meat loaf, then says, "I'm meeting up with some of the other calendar guys to celebrate. Your dad's at work."

My dad is a ranger at Huntsville State Park. "When is he going to be home?" I ask.

"Late. He's doing a full moon nature hike out at the park."

No surprise. I am going to be alone again. It happens more and more these days.

(X) (♥) (X)

After Mom leaves, I hang out in the living room, scrolling through my phone with the empty cereal bowl beside me. It is so quiet—so different from the home I used to know with a mom and a brother and a dad.

Now there's just me.

I pull up the Hornet and frown down at it. The *Write New Post* button taunts me. The air conditioner kicks in with a muffled mechanical rattle and I hear Bonnie Raitt singing softly in the next room: *"Let's give them something to talk about."* My mom left the radio on. I don't get up to turn it off, though—too much trouble.

Murphy settles onto the couch beside me, his head in my lap. I look down into his golden eyes, and his chocolate furry eyebrows lift in question. Listening is one of Murphy's strengths. Even as a puppy, he was determined to be by my side. On the first night he came home with us, he was supposed to sleep on the floor in my room in a newly purchased doggy bed. But even then, he had a mind of his own. Gradually he learned to put his giant, too-big-for-his-puppy-body paws on the mattress and peer over the edge. Then finally, against all the rules, he learned to pull his chunk of a body over the top of the mattress and snuggle deep into the covers, where he stayed all night long. Right at my fingertips.

Eventually, I would talk to him.

And the dog would listen. Sometimes with his eyelids

so heavy he could barely keep them up. Sometimes lying on his back, his pink lake of a tummy exposed for belly rubs. And other times, when my voice cracked with all the emotion of my middle school drama, he lay right on top of my chest—one paw on each shoulder, dog heart to person heart—and stared right into my eyes.

We are both older now. Murphy is no longer a puppy, but he is still a great listener. His blocky head is heavy in my lap and he rolls his eyes up to look at my face.

"So what do you think I should do about this prom publicity thing?" I ask him, angling my phone toward him so he can see the screen. It's not a cat video, so he's not interested.

"You're a good dog," I say, and Murphy's tail thumps against the couch at the sound of my voice. Everything is so simple in his world. "You know exactly why you're here on this planet. Not everyone does."

I scratch his ears in just the right place and Murphy grins his happy smile, tongue hanging out the side of his mouth. Then his eyes close and within minutes, I hear little doggy snores.

Careful not to disturb him, I turn the phone back toward me. Unfortunately, no words magically typed themselves onto the Hornet. I do a quick Google search for "prom." Most of the hits are for dresses and makeup tips. I read a *Teen Vogue* article on "swoon-worthy" dresses and then sit, staring off into space. My mother would be horrified that

I'm spending my evening supporting the prom industry and female stereotypes.

I have a quick idea and log in to Instagram. In a flurry of keystrokes, I post some photos of gorgeous models wearing the latest in prom fashions, and I tag Jayla, Taylor, and all the other Lovelies. I comment on how much the photos remind me of them. #sogorgeous #promqueens

Within minutes, there are likes and new followers. When the shares start, I know I've hit on something. Now is the time to put my writing skills to use.

I log back in to the Hornet and write:

"You are cordially invited to the Huntsville High School prom. A ticket to your perfect Enchanted Evening is on sale now in the main office. Due to the amazing fundraising efforts of the junior class, the price of admission is only $40.00 per person and includes party favors, a buffet dinner, and dancing. Music will be provided by the awesome local band The Barneys. Don't miss out on the biggest night of your life!"

Smiling, I sink back into the couch cushions, surveying my work. It isn't the next best seller, but it's a start to launching my own identity. Maybe this isn't going to be that hard after all.

I open Facebook to read my newsfeed and then check Twitter. Max is right. Everyone from school is talking about Worthy.

Did you guys download this app? It's crazy!

Omg will Taylor be worthy?

Have y'all voted yet?

My precalculus homework isn't going to magically finish itself, but before I reach into my bag for my textbook, I open the app.

The photo of Taylor and Liam, and all the comments, are still there. But something is different now. The *yes/no* buttons are gone, and there is a spinning ball over Taylor's face.

And then, just like that, the results pop up on the screen.

Congratulations, Taylor!

85% say YES!

You are WORTHY!

Swipe here for more!

No big surprise that Taylor is worthy, I suppose. I swipe on the screen, and new words pop up:

Hey, Hornets! Word is a new couple is headed to the spotlight. When one hundred people have downloaded the app, the next photo will be posted.

Share and share alike. You be the judge.

"Now what happens? Is that it?" I ask Murphy. He opens his eyes to look up at me, then closes them again. It's obviously way past his bedtime.

He's got no answers, and neither do I.

CHAPTER FIVE

I arrive at the baseball field on Thursday afternoon feeling beyond nervous. As Nikki suggested, I'm wearing boyfriend jeans, a tank top, and the white wrap sweater.

I squint and look out onto the field to see if I can find Alex. Rows of players are out there, warming up. There is the occasional sound of a bat cracking into a ball as the coach hits flies for the outfielders. I hear the rhythmic pop of the balls landing in gloves.

I shield the sun from my eyes and see Alex. He is walking toward the backstop with his baseball glove in one hand. He looks really handsome in his uniform and my heartbeat speeds up. I don't think he's seen me yet. If he looks up toward the crowd, I'll wave, just to let him know I'm here.

The bleachers are crazy crowded, but I manage to squeeze down the row to an empty spot halfway up. When I glance around to see if I recognize anyone, I'm surprised. Everybody who's anybody at Huntsville High School is here—even a couple of cheerleaders who usually only show up to support the football team. They must have heard the rumors that, after years of dismal losing streaks, this baseball team might actually be good enough to make it to the championships. Everyone likes winners.

I sit by myself in front of a group of freshman girls. To distract myself, I pull out my phone. Almost automatically, I open Worthy.

I gasp. A new couple is up today. There's a picture of Raylene Anderson and her boyfriend, Ross, standing in the school parking lot. Raylene's bleach blonde hair is teased up into a big bump on the back of her head and she's wearing her twirler outfit. Ross has on his football uniform. He's a couple of inches shorter than her, but he has his arm draped around her shoulders and she is smiling down at him. It's a cute photo, but I'm a little surprised. Raylene isn't in the same crowd as Taylor and her friends. It makes me wonder how these couples are being selected and who is behind it all.

The question underneath the photo is the same as last time: "Is she worthy?"

I think back to what Kat said, about why the app singled out the girl instead of the guy. I close out of the app and glance back to the field. I see that Alex has stopped to talk to a couple: Torrey Grey and her boyfriend, Luis Rivera.

Right. I remember that Luis and Alex are cousins. With the two of them standing side by side, I can see they are definitely related. Both have the same dark hair and dark skin, but Luis is taller and bigger. He also seems so much more serious than Alex. I've rarely seen him smile or laugh. Alex, on the other hand, is laughing right now. His eyes half closed and his head thrown back into the sunlight. It makes me want to be there by his side listening to how wonderful that laugh sounds.

I'm distracted by the voices of the freshman girls sitting behind me.

"Did you vote for Raylene today?"

"Yeah. I voted *no*! I don't know what Ross sees in her. I mean, she's pretty, I guess, but she's so weird . . ."

". . . He's just using her until someone better comes along . . ."

". . . Maybe she's not that bad . . ."

I'm speechless. Freshmen are voting on Worthy now? Has it gotten that big already?

". . . It's all about image. The person you're with can make or break you. Raylene definitely knows that. Maybe she's not as ditzy as she acts . . ."

"A popular guy with a girl like that and all of a sudden you look at him a little differently, you know?"

"I always thought he was cute; now I'm not so sure . . ."

I try to tune them out. Down at the fence, I see Alex wave to Luis and Torrey, and he walks off toward the dugout. I watch as two umpires gather in a tight circle around second base, laughing and talking. The game must be about to begin.

First-string pitcher Chance Lehmann is on the mound, slapping his fist into his glove and waiting for Alex to finish putting on all his gear. Crouching down on the ground behind home plate, Alex puts on his glove and holds it up for the first pitch. The ball pops into his glove in a blur of power. Alex stands to throw it back, hard and fast, and my heart swells with pride.

"Anybody sitting here?" Taylor Reed is suddenly standing beside me. She is wearing her blonde hair in big fat braids and her pale, long legs are shown off to perfection in a floral, high-necked skater dress. Jayla stands at her side, wearing a scarf tied around the top of her head, leaving the rest of her hair curling wildly around her shoulders. Shimmery gold eye shadow, black eyeliner, and berry-stained lips add a hint of glamour to her otherwise dressed-down outfit of jeans, T-shirt, and a black duster that brushes the tops of her Chelsea boots. She and Taylor make a formidable duo of prom queen wannabes. Thank God I have no such aspirations.

Behind us, the freshmen girls are quietly squealing, punching one another, and pointing at Taylor and Jayla.

I pick up my backpack and put it at my feet to clear the spot. "Nope. All yours."

"Thanks." Taylor plops down onto the bench with a clink of jewelry and a cloud of perfume. I cough as the sweetness envelops me, but she doesn't seem to notice. Instead, she drapes an arm over my shoulders and squeezes me tightly into her side. "This is the girl that's going to make us all look good," she announces to no one in particular. I guess she's referring to the prom publicity stuff.

No pressure or anything.

We sit like that for a few beats—me choking on the smell and her hugging. *Awkward.* Finally, I pull myself out of her grasp and scoot away for space enough to breathe.

Jayla leans forward to smile at me. "Hey, I saw your mom made the firefighter calendar. My cousin is at her firehouse. He says she's great."

"Thanks," I stammer back, surprised she's talking to me and even more shocked she actually knows about my mom.

Unfazed, she grins at me. "So you're here to watch Alex?" she asks.

News gets out fast, but I'm not going to deny it. "Yeah."

"He's really good. I hear college scouts are already looking at him. By the end of baseball season, he's going to be the hottest thing around. Everybody will be talking about him."

I glance over at her to make sure she's serious. She is, and my stomach flips as I laugh nervously. I don't want everyone knowing that Alex is "the hottest thing around." It's my secret.

Sitting up a little straighter, I watch Alex behind the plate. This time the ball comes in fast and too low. It bounces into the dirt in front of him, then off to the side. He dives for it, but it gets past him and rattles back against the fence.

"Hustle, Alex!" the coach yells across the infield. "Don't let those get away from you. You never know when a runner might be on third just waiting for that kind of mistake."

Alex picks up the ball and throws it back to the pitcher, then squats down and slaps his glove with his fist.

Suddenly, Taylor stands up, waving wildly and yelling. "Torrey! Hey, Torrey . . . "

Torrey Grey is sitting farther down in the stands with Luis. She looks up at Taylor and waves back. Taylor sits down again and fiddles with her braid.

"Torrey's been really supporting me with this whole Worthy thing," she whispers to me. "She knows what it's like to be bullied online."

Taylor seems upset, and I'm surprised. She was voted *worthy*. And she got more attention. Isn't that all she would care about?

The freshmen sitting behind us are silent, listening. I can feel them leaning in closer to hear better. Taylor now has their complete attention. I should warn her about the nosy busybodies, but I'm not sure how to do it without them hearing.

Jayla looks down at her phone. "Three different people just texted me about Worthy since we've been sitting here. It's out of control."

"I just don't understand. Why me?" Taylor crosses her arms and stares down at the field.

"Why not you?" Jayla asks. I'm surprised at the bitterness in her voice. "Girls are trained for this kind of scrutiny from the time we are little. People tell us if we're pretty . . . or thin . . . or smart."

"And they tell us if we're not any of those things,"

I say, because I've already read some of the comments under Raylene and Ross's picture.

Then the game starts and I try to pay attention, but my thoughts about Worthy, and Taylor, and Raylene, and Alex are swirling around. When Alex comes up to bat, the crowd breaks out in a roar. I look around in shock. They're all cheering for him. For Alex. It gives me goose bumps and a weird unsettled feeling in the pit of my stomach.

The game is close and the tension high on the field and in the stands. At the top of the eighth inning, they are tied.

Alex stands up behind the plate to yell at the pitcher, "Come on, Chance. One more out."

But even before the ball leaves Chance's hand, everyone knows the first base runner is going to steal second. The batter swings wildly. It is a diversion, but Alex isn't distracted. He catches the ball, stands up, and throws it hard, directly toward a spot where there is no one to catch it. Alex's arm is strong and his aim perfect. The shortstop arrives at just the right moment to hold out his glove, snatch the ball out of the air, and in an almost seamless movement, tag the sliding runner from first base.

"Out!" shouts the umpire, and the crowd goes wild. Taylor jumps up and down beside me, yelling like a banshee.

"Way to go, Alex," she cups her hands over her mouth and yells.

Jayla claps and cheers and gives me a smile, like I have something to be proud of now.

After the game, Alex is surrounded by cheering teammates congratulating him, so I wait for him at the fence.

"Hey," Alex says when he sees me.

"You were fantastic. I had no idea you were so . . .
good." It was such an understatement. "Congrats."

"Thanks." He pulls up his shirt and wipes the sweat off
his forehead. My breath catches in my throat at the defini-
tion in his abs. Behind him, the freshmen girls from the
bleachers are giggling and watching. They definitely aren't
scrutinizing me. Just Alex and his sculpted stomach. It's
all I can do not to reach out and yank his shirt back down.

Chance Lehmann and Lucas Murray, the first baseman,
come out the gate. Chance slaps Alex on the back. "Good
game," he says.

"Thanks." Alex grins at him. "You were great, too."

"You guys are unstoppable," Lucas says.

"Some of us are going out now. You want to come?"
Chance asks Alex. He doesn't seem to realize I'm standing
there with Alex, or maybe he just doesn't care. "We're
thinking about going to Jilly's and then over to my house.
Some girls might drop by later. Like Taylor Reed."

"Did you hear she broke up with Liam?" Lucas says,
and I'm stunned. Is *that* why Taylor seemed upset in the
stands? "After the Worthy vote sank in," Lucas goes on,
"she must have thought she could do even better. I'm
thinking I might even ask her out."

"I guess they weren't the perfect couple after all," I say, the thought spilling out before I can stop it.

"So, you're coming, right?" Chance gestures for Alex to follow him to the parking lot, but Alex shakes his head.

"Sorry, Chance," he says. "I can't today. Maybe next time?"

After a couple more shoves and arm punches, the boys leave. I hope Alex is not regretting his decision to stay behind with me. He picks up his athletic bag off the dirt and swings it over one shoulder. Why haven't I ever noticed those muscles in his arms before? I've been so blind. He looks at me with a half smile.

"You okay?"

I release a slow breath. "I am now."

"How about that snow cone?" he asks me, and I nod.

We walk over to the concession stand. I order a grape one from the middle school girl behind the counter. She smiles at Alex, revealing a mouth full of braces.

"Not pickle juice?" Alex asks me when the girl hands over the purple mound of ice.

I gasp. "Is that really a thing?"

"Yep. My sister's favorite. They just pour the juice off those pickles"—he points to the big jar on the countertop—"right over the shaved ice."

"No, thanks." I make a horrified face that makes him laugh. "Your sister, Isabella, she's a freshman, right?" I ask him.

He nods, taking a bite of his strawberry snow cone.

"I've seen her around. She's cute."

He nods again. "Her fifteenth birthday is coming up and she's having a huge party. It's a big thing in Mexican families."

"A *quinceañera*? I've heard of it, but haven't ever gone to one. It's sort of like a sweet sixteen party?" I ask.

"Yes, but with a church blessing. The party will be after the mass."

"And it will be big?"

"Enormous. Izzy is having fourteen *damas* . . . attendants . . . and each one of them will have an escort called a *chambelan*. One for each year of her life," he says. "And that's just the beginning."

"Wow. That's going to be quite the party."

He nods. "We're having it out at Magnolia Lake."

"I went to a wedding reception there once. It was beautiful."

He grimaces. "Yeah. My family is going all out on this party."

"You don't look that happy about it," I say.

"It's all-consuming. I'll be glad when it's over."

We take our snow cones over to the now half-empty bleachers and sit down. I want to say something, but being together outside of the library feels different. This is Alex's world. It makes me long for my comfort zone deep in the book stacks, far away from cheering crowds and baseball fields. I want to be noticed, but I can't imagine what it would feel like to have every eye on me while I put a book on the shelf and then, if I do it just right, for the watching crowd to break out in wild cheers. I take a bite of the ice and hold it on my tongue until it melts.

Finally, Alex breaks the silence and asks, "Want to taste?"

He holds out his red snow cone. I lean in to take a small bite, but I can't stop looking at him. The ice breaks away into sticky red chunks under my lips and drips down my chin. I cover my mouth with my hand, trying to catch the slippery mess before it lands on my shirt.

"Sorry. I'm a mess," I say, then laugh.

Alex doesn't laugh. "You missed a spot." He brushes a thumb against the corner of my mouth, leaving a trail of tingling skin behind. Heat bubbles up my neck.

"Thanks," I whisper.

Time freezes.

Then he clears his throat and the trance is broken. He looks away toward the baseball field and I look down toward our feet. His cleats are covered in the chalk from the batting box.

"So what's your favorite summer food? Ice cream, Popsicles, watermelon?" I'm sure his question is meant to cut through the awkwardness, and I'm grateful.

I think for a minute. "S'mores. My family used to go tent camping every vacation and the campfire was my favorite part."

"Even when it was hot?"

"Yes. My dad was kind of obsessive about it. He's a park

ranger out at Huntsville State Park and being outside was always his thing. It wasn't a camping trip until my dad made a fire and we roasted marshmallows . . . "

"And made s'mores." Alex smiles.

I nod. "It's probably about the memory rather than the actual food."

Then he tells me about his *abuela*'s tamales, which they have every Christmas Eve, and says, "Sometimes the best food is all wrapped up in memories."

"Exactly," I say, and my heart kind of flips over.

We sit for a moment, eating our snow cones in silence, but I'm not uncomfortable with it anymore.

"So does your family still go camping?" Alex asks. There is a tiny piece of strawberry ice on his bottom lip that suddenly fascinates me.

I swallow hard, trying to focus on the conversation and not on his mouth. "No. My mom has this new job. She's a firefighter," I tell him. "It's a lot of work right now and she doesn't get off much."

"And you miss those family vacations."

I glance over at him and then say, "You just made me realize I do."

"I guess I'm good for something," he says with a half smile.

"You're good at a lot of things," I say. I look down at the purple streak melting down my hand from the snow cone, then back up to meet his eyes.

"Like what?"

"Like baseball," I say, licking a bit of sticky grape off my thumb.

"I've been waiting for my turn to start for a while now. The coaches always play the seniors first, but it's been hard watching from the bench," he says. "I think it surprised everyone how hard I've been working on the off season."

"Now it's your turn to shine."

"I'm not letting anything go to my head. It's only one game and there's a whole season left. Besides, there's always someone waiting in the wings who is better," he says, and I see a muscle twitch in his jaw. "I think that's why I hate running so much. It's never enough. There's always faster. Even when it's only one second. That one second is better."

I realize he's opening up to me, showing a different side of himself. "When you hit that finish line and realize you ran the fastest ever, there's still another second faster," he continues, looking over at me. "It isn't the *best*."

"I feel that way sometimes," I say. "Like I'll never be good enough."

"What do you want to be good at?" he asks.

I think for a minute. "Writing," I say, surprised I've said it out loud. "It's kind of a dream of mine."

He smiles. "Really? That's so cool. Why do you love writing?"

I chew on my lip for a minute, tasting the cold, before I answer. "In real life, it's hard to really see through someone else's eyes. But I can do that when I'm writing. I can be in their head, seeing what they see, hearing what they hear. And sometimes I notice things. Little things." I point to a spot above center field. "Like that perfectly white line across the blue sky means there was a plane there not long ago. I wonder where it's going and who is on board."

Alex looks up to find the streak in the sky. "I didn't even see that."

"Most people don't." I shrug. "I can't really explain it, but my brain just wants to put words around all those things."

"I'd love to read one of your stories." Alex must sense my reluctance, because then he adds, "If it's okay."

I laugh, shaking my head. "Sorry. I like to write stories, but I'm not very good at letting other people read them. I want to . . . but . . . " I look out at the pitcher's mound and change the subject. "What do you like about baseball?" I ask him. "It seems like a lot of pressure to play that well in front of such a huge crowd." *Kind of like showing my writing to the world,* I think. "I don't know how you do it."

"Being a catcher is probably the most dangerous position on the field," Alex says thoughtfully. "Not only do you have the ball flying at you like a streak of lightning, but you also have that batter standing just inches away from your outstretched glove. I don't think about it anymore. It's all instinct. I squat down behind the plate, and somehow I know exactly how much space I need between me and that swinging bat. I know exactly where to move my glove when I see the ball leave the pitcher's hand." He looks over at me. "It's instinct and lots of practice."

"And talent."

He laughs. "But I make mistakes. A lot of them. Sometimes I get a little too close to the batter, and when the bat swings around it catches my glove." He shrugs. "But I know I'm going to put that hand right back in that glove, squat down, and keep playing no matter how much it hurts."

I feel myself relax, leaning back against the bench behind me. Before I know it, I say, "I volunteered to be in charge of the prom publicity. Like posting to the Hornet and stuff."

He stares at me, the snow cone halfway to his mouth; then he says, "That sounds like fun."

But he says it in a way that doesn't seem like he thinks it's fun at all, and then he changes the subject really fast. "Are you working at the library tomorrow? I thought I'd drop by before practice and check out another audiobook . . . "

I nod and take another slushy bite, glancing down at Alex's dirt-covered cleats. I don't tell him he can download the books from the library's website because I really want to see him again. Withholding that information probably breaks some kind of librarian code or something, but I'm not sorry.

"Great," he says. "I'll see you then. And, um . . . "

I can feel him looking at me. I glance at him, waiting.

"Would you like to go out with me on Saturday night?"

I suck in my breath so hard, I almost choke. The lobes of his ears are pink again, but his eyes don't look away.

I cough a little, then gather myself together. A smile spreads across my face.

"Yes," I say. "I would love to go out with you."

CHAPTER SIX

"I could get you a job at Sephora," Nikki says. It's Friday afternoon and we're walking through the school parking lot together. "That way you'd always have enough makeup in advance of all your dates with Alex."

I laugh. "So far it's only *one* date with Alex," I point out. My stomach jumps. That date—our first real date—is happening tomorrow night.

Tomorrow night!

"Well, Sephora's more fun than the library," Nikki argues.

The new Sephora just opened out by the highway and Nikki is the makeover queen at the front desk. I hate the stereotype that girls can't like makeup *and* books, because I love both. I just love books more.

"I adore working at the library," I say. She rolls her eyes at me. Nikki has never understood my passion for books and writing. It's the one thing she and I don't agree on. I've tried to explain that books are as meaningful to me as fashion is to her, but she just can't see it.

Every summer, when I was growing up, the library had

those contests to encourage kids to read. I finished all my books before most got through the first one. I came back so often the librarian finally offered me a job. At first it was a part-time job, just volunteering, but it soon became a paying one when I turned sixteen last summer. I do my homework during the slow times and they are really flexible with my hours. But the best thing is to be surrounded by those walls and walls of books. It makes me smile to think of it.

"Is Alex coming to the library this afternoon?"

"Maybe," I say, but I think *yes.* The thought is enough to make my toes curl up inside my boots. My smile turns into a huge grin.

"You got it bad," Nikki says. I don't disagree because, well, it's true. And Nikki knows it. There isn't anything I can hide from her. She knows all my secrets. And I know all of hers. Or at least I thought I did until Jake came along. I never saw that one coming.

We stop to wait for a car to drive out of the lane in front of us. Heather is at the wheel, and she waves at us like we are best friends. Then Nikki and I keep walking, weaving in and out of the cars still left in the spaces.

I say, "I don't even know what this is going to be with me and Alex yet." Which is true. I only have the memory of our eating snow cones together, and then my hopes for tomorrow night.

"But you like him?" She knows I do; she just wants me to say it out loud.

"Yes."

"Boyfriend kind of like him? Or go-to-the-movies-and-hold-hands kind of like him?"

"How do I know?" I ask, fumbling for my keys in my bag. "Nothing has happened yet. No movies. No hand holding . . ."

"No kissing?" she asks.

My heart skips a beat. "Nothing."

We stop at Nikki's car, a silver Prius with a big dent in the back passenger door. She opens the driver's door and slides in, turning on the engine. "Yet," she says, grinning at me.

I know I'm blushing as I wave good-bye. Then I keep walking across the parking lot toward my beat-up Chevy truck.

Jayla and Taylor are standing by the driver's side of my truck, looking down at their phones. These two have never been this chummy before, but with the prom queen competition coming up, they seem to be inseparable. I guess it's all about keeping friends close, but frenemies even closer. The prom campaign has kicked into high gear and neither leading candidate is willing to leave the other alone to implement sneaky, vote-swaying tricks.

The girls ignore me completely, but they're blocking my driver's door, so I'm going to have to say something. My truck looks really bad next to Taylor's red Volkswagen convertible, but at least it's reliable.

"So, spill. Did you vote yes or no for Raylene?" I hear Taylor ask Jayla when I get closer.

"It's *supposed* to be a secret ballot," Jayla snaps. She finally looks up and acknowledges me. "Hey."

"Hey. Sorry." I point at my truck. "I need to get to work."

"Have you voted yet?" Taylor asks me. She holds up her phone to show Worthy on the screen.

"No," I say, which is half true. I haven't voted on Raylene and Ross. But I did vote on Taylor and Liam. I helped her win the overwhelmingly positive endorsement of their relationship. The relationship that is apparently now over.

Taylor glances back down at her phone. "I get why everyone has an opinion, but why was *Raylene* selected? Seriously?"

"What's wrong with Raylene?" I ask.

"Nothing," Taylor tells me. "She's just not in the same league as . . . " She pauses and looks sideways at Jayla. ". . . us."

Potential prom queens? Chosen ones?

"Raylene has just as much of a right to be on that app as any of us," Jayla says. I realize how crazy it is to be arguing for an opportunity to be judged by the whole school.

"You're right. You're always right. Has anyone ever told you how annoying it is?" Taylor tucks one long strand of blonde hair behind one ear and taps away at her phone. "There. I voted."

"Good," Jayla says, but I'm not sure it is. I would bet Taylor voted *no*. It's clear she doesn't deem Raylene worthy.

Taylor finally looks up at me, studying my face. "You're so much prettier when you smile, Linden. You should try it."

Evidently, I'm an annoying know-it-all and have a face that says I don't care about anything. It's not a surprise. I should be used to it by now. My grandmother used to say the sun came out when I smiled. It was a much nicer way of pointing out that my usual expression is pretty solemn. My brother shares the exact face-altering smile as I do— but no one insists he use it constantly.

Taylor doesn't know anything about me. I care. I care a lot.

I plaster on a smile and point at the door of my truck. "Excuse me?" I remind them.

They shuffle out of the way—barely—and I squeeze by.

"Will you vote yes or no?" Taylor asks me, and my hand stops midway to the door handle.

"I don't know," I admit, though what I really should say is *It's none of your business*.

"Do it now," Taylor says. "I'll show you how."

"It's okay. I can figure it out," I say, pulling open the door to the truck. The guilt burns up into my cheeks, but I don't admit I already know how to use the app.

Taylor steps in between me and the driver's seat. "Let's see."

"Fine." I take out my phone and pull up Worthy. Neither of them seems surprised I already have it downloaded. I click the heart under the picture and hold it up for them to see. "Happy?"

Taylor makes a face. "Are you *sure* that's the way you want to vote?"

"Positive," I say, and climb up into the truck, slamming the door behind me.

It's a particularly slow day at the circulation desk, so Kat tells me her dream of joining a roller derby team and I tell her I want to enter the writing contest. She doesn't laugh or tell me I'm crazy. She just says, "Cool. Your main character can be in the roller derby, and her name can be Kat Killzem."

I roll my eyes but secretly think it is awesome, and I write it down in my journal for some future character reference.

Everything about Kat is smooth and dark, from the top of her jet-black hair to the tip of her black motorcycle boots. When she isn't at the library, she hangs out with other übercool girls and watches her boyfriend, Teo, play the drums in a local jazz band called Serendipity. I heard the band a couple of times on Saturday nights at the local coffee shop, and they're great.

There are rumors that Kat is an elite computer hacker

and already has a full-ride scholarship to MIT. It could definitely be true, but there are a lot of rumors about Kat. She is totally the kind of person I could write a story about. A story that would be edgy and brazen and wildly popular.

The front door of the library finally opens and I look up hopefully. It's just Mr. Hooper. He comes to the library every day about now to look at magazines before the Cyber Senior class starts. I look back down, picking up my pen and drawing a big circle in the margin of my journal.

Where's Alex?

Cyber Seniors is a group that connects teenage mentors with older people who want to learn about using the internet. Kat saw a documentary about two sisters who began Cyber Seniors for a school project. She talked Mrs. Longshore, the librarian, into trying it out in our library. It makes me feel good to see how happy Mr. Hooper is to Skype with his grandkids in New York, and Mrs. Pirtle's YouTube video on rose gardening already has ten views. Most of those views are from other Cyber Seniors, but she is still feeling stoked about the whole thing. I think that's what the internet should be about. Not judging people's significance with snarky comments. But I'm obviously in the minority.

Take Worthy, for example. The comments on Raylene's page have skyrocketed since my conversation with Taylor, and the cruel remarks are piling up.

Not that I'm checking.

"Is April's *Vogue* here?" Mr. Hooper asks, walking up to the desk. He is about eighty or so, bald except for two tufts of gray hair above each ear and one long, thin strand he combs over from one side to the other.

"I think it's over on the stand," I say.

Then he says, and I recite it along with him—but just in my head, because it would be rude to say it aloud: "You know, I used to live right in downtown Manhattan."

"That must have been fun," I say, but I don't really know because I've never lived anywhere else but Huntsville, Texas.

"I had an apartment right by Central Park. I could see the horses and carriages from my window."

According to all the books I've read set in New York, I know you can't see Central Park from downtown Manhattan. But I don't correct him. Over his shoulder, the clock says 4:45 p.m.

Mr. Hooper pulls out a box of green Tic Tacs from his pocket and rattles them. "Mint?" he asks.

I shake my head. Mr. Hooper carefully pours out two mints and pops them in his mouth. He shifts his weight over to his left foot and stands there, waiting for me to say something.

I could ask him a lot of questions about New York. I know it's what he wants. Mr. Hooper has great stories about the restaurants and the museums and the people. Usually, I am fascinated. But today my mind is on other things. So I just smile and look back down at my journal.

When I look up again, Mr. Hooper is still standing there, Tic Tacs in hand.

"*Vogue* is right over there." I motion toward the magazine racks on the back wall and feel a twinge of guilt when he shuffles reluctantly off in that direction. I know how much he loves to talk.

The next time the door opens, it is Mrs. Pirtle. She is wearing a blue-jean hat with a button on top that says, "I have cancer. My husband is just bald." Mrs. Pirtle also likes to come a bit early for the Cyber Senior meetings and read the paper out loud to me. At first, I tried to ignore her. Politely, of course. I mean, I don't want to be rude to people with cancer . . . or really anyone. But Mrs. Pirtle was persistent, and the stories in her paper were always unusual, to say the least. It didn't matter how busy the desk was, or how much I obviously had to do, she still read to me about the boa constrictor that escaped from his cage in California and ate a small dog, or about the man who tried to fly away with helium balloons strapped to his lawn chair. And since I am definitely a sucker for a good story, Mrs. Pirtle's paper reading is now a familiar habit.

Today, Mrs. Pirtle settles in at the table next to my desk and opens her newspaper with a flourish. She announces the location of the news story first. "Buenos Aires, Argentina."

Kat and I exchange a knowing glance. *Here we go.*

"Statue of Rabbit Cures Toe Fungus." Mrs. Pirtle reads the headline aloud, and keeps reading. All about the statue and how people who touched it were miraculously healed of all kinds of foot-related issues.

"I thought the only kind of statues that did miracles like that were in churches," I say as I draw a few flowers in the corner of my journal.

She looks up from the paper to give me a very serious glare over the top of her purple reading glasses. "Maybe this rabbit statue was made at the same place as those religious statues that heal people, and it rubbed off."

"I don't think it works that way," I say doubtfully, but then think maybe a healing rabbit statue is just what Mrs. Pirtle needs. "But I guess you never know."

I look back at the clock.

Five p.m.

Maybe he isn't coming. My mother would say I'm turning into one of those girls whose world revolves around a guy. And I know that is bad. Very bad.

Mrs. Pirtle stops reading, and I look over at the sudden silence. She is looking back toward the magazine rack. "Maybe Mr. Hooper knows something about rabbit statues. He lived in New York, and they have all kinds of statues there."

"Could be," I say, not wanting to put a damper on her rabbit statue story, but really not in the mood for more today. "Why don't you go ask him?"

She nods, picks up her paper, and heads off toward the far wall. I resist looking back at the clock.

"Ever heard the expression, a watched pot never boils?" Kat asks from beside me, flipping through a recently returned book.

I kick myself mentally for underestimating her. Of course she knows. Even so, I still try to act like I don't have a clue. "Huh?"

"He'll get here," Kat says.

"Who?" I ask, and she rolls her eyes at me.

Then, with perfect timing, the front doors open, and Alex Rivera walks into the library. He smiles at me across the room and I smile back, then look down at the desk like I am really busy. I don't want him to see the feeling that just burst up into my cheeks, making them hot and pink. This is like the worst scene in every romantic comedy ever. Cue sappy music.

Kat snorts a laugh under her breath.

"Hey," he says when he gets to the desk. "Sorry I'm late."

"Hey," I say back.

"Finally," Kat says. I kick her under the desk.

"Ouch," she says, rubbing her ankle.

"Aren't you supposed to finish story time?" I say to Kat. She leaves with a grin and a stack of picture books, giving me a thumbs-up sign.

"I'm going to go back there and work on my homework." Alex points to the study area in the corner. "Maybe you can come over when you get a break?"

I nod. "I'm leading Cyber Seniors. I'll come over when I finish."

"What's that?" Alex asks.

"It's a study group for older people. I teach them all about the internet," I tell him. "Today I'm teaching Mrs. Pirtle how to use Facebook."

Alex laughs. "Cool. Come find me when you're done."

I race through Cyber Seniors, then go to the back of the library. I find Alex at a table, an open book and a notebook in front of him. I slide into the seat beside him. He looks down at his notepad quickly, like he's actually doing homework. The cold air that pours out of the air-conditioning vent in the ceiling ruffles at the pages of the math book in front of us, but neither of us is interested in math. I can see Alex sneaking looks over at me.

I look at him, too, when I think he doesn't know—short glances out of the corners of my eyes that take in his thick, straight black hair and the sharpness of his cheekbones. Sometimes he looks up at just the wrong—or right?—moment, and I'm caught, heart in my eyes. Instantly, my throat turns red and blotchy at the hint of possibility in his dark eyes.

"How'd Cyber Seniors go?" he finally asks. "Did you help Mrs. Pirtle with Facebook?"

"I think so. She sent you a friend request. Will you accept it so she can see how it works?"

He smiles. "Sure." He speaks very softly. Almost a whisper.

"What?" I lean in and then say a little louder, "Why are you talking like that?"

"It's a library," he hisses, then grins. Those braces in eighth grade definitely did their job. His teeth are impossibly white and straight. "You're supposed to be quiet."

"Library stereotype," I say. "The good news is that you don't have to be that quiet here, or else Kat would have been kicked out a long time ago."

Alex reaches out to flip the page back at the same time that I move to do the same. Our hands touch and electricity sparks through my fingers. I pull away, but don't know what to do with that hand now, so I awkwardly push my glasses back up my nose for the third time since I sat down. I should have put my contacts in today. Nikki's always telling me to take more time getting ready in the morning.

"Did you finish *To Kill a Mockingbird*?" I ask him.

He nods enthusiastically. "I finished a 5K because I had to keep listening. Thanks for the help."

"I'm glad you liked it."

"More than liked it," he says. "It was awesome. Actually," Alex adds, looking sheepish, "I know it's due back soon. I should have brought it today."

I wave my hand. "You have time. You said you wanted

to check out another book, right?" He nods. "What's your next assignment for English?"

Alex smiles. "Well, I finished *To Kill a Mockingbird* so fast that we don't even have our next book assigned yet. I was thinking I'd listen to one just . . . for fun."

I laugh at how surprised he sounds at this. "Do you not usually think of books as fun?" I ask.

He shakes his head. "I've never been much of a reader. I hate to admit it. Especially to you."

I feel a flutter of pleasure and embarrassment. "Why would you care what I think?"

He gives me a look, like I should know better.

"I was always a slow reader," he explains softly, "so then I became incredibly self-conscious about it. Avoided it mostly. Listening to these books made me realize how much I missed." He's studying me with eyes so dark I can't tell where the pupils start and end. The corner of his mouth twitches up into a half smile.

"I can't imagine not having books in my life," I say. "I guess that's why I want to write one someday."

"That's so cool, Linden," he says, and I can tell he means it. There is something in his expression that keeps me from looking away. It doesn't matter that kids are running around in the story area, squealing and laughing. Or that the returned books are piling up in the bin waiting to be reshelved. Or that Kat keeps glancing over and making googly-eyed faces. None of it matters.

"So, um," I say, trying to break the spell, "I'm thinking maybe next you should listen to *The Hitchhiker's Guide to the Galaxy*. Have you ever read it?"

He shakes his head. "I've heard of it, but no. Didn't they make it into a movie?"

I can't help but smile at the wonder of introducing a newbie. "Don't even go there," I say. "The book is always better."

Okay, I'm a nerd, but this happens every time I recommend an incredible book to someone who hasn't read it before.

Alex laughs. "I'll try it."

"I can't wait to talk to you about it. I'll put the audiobook up at the checkout desk for you."

"Thanks," Alex says. Then, after a pause, he clears his throat and asks, "We're still on for tomorrow?"

I nod, and just for a second I forget to breathe. "What's the plan?"

"It's a surprise," Alex says.

My nerves prickle. I'm not a big fan of surprises. It's hard to make a foolproof plan when things are uncertain.

I hesitate, but say, "Sounds good," because it would be crazy to insist on him spoiling the surprise because I need to know what kind of shoes to wear.

"I should get to practice," Alex says, closing his book and stuffing it into his backpack.

"I'll get that audiobook for you," I say. I stand up too, picking up his notebook and handing it to him. I notice it

is completely blank. He gives me a smile, closing the notebook. But his fingers linger on mine, and this time I don't
pull my hand away. Fingers entwined, I notice how the dark
brown of his fingers contrasts with my own pale skin.
Different, but perfect together. I let out a breath.

CHAPTER SEVEN

On Saturday night, I stop at the bottom of the stairs to yell back down the entryway to my mom and the group of firemen sitting in our living room. "I'm leaving!"

Bobby Lewis, one of the fire chiefs, yells back, "Don't we get to meet this guy?" His question is followed by loud laughter, and I curse under my breath. This is exactly what I was hoping to avoid.

I stand in front of the hallway mirror, putting on a final swipe of lip gloss. My hand shakes a little from nerves, but somehow I manage to keep my Bobbi Brown Pink Lily gloss on my lips and not all over my chin.

With lots of advice from Nikki, I decided to wear a little black dress with a scoop neck and flutter sleeves. It's cute and flirty—not something I'd normally wear, but tonight seems like the night for it. I paired it with my red cowboy boots, which I kind of think of as good-luck shoes, since I was wearing them the day Alex first came to the library. My hair is curled into beachy waves that took way longer to style than I planned. Looking into the mirror now,

though, I think the time spent was totally worth it. I practice a smile, remembering what Taylor said. Nobody is
going to think I look too serious tonight.

There is another roar of laughter from the living room
and I cringe, putting the cap back on the gloss and sliding it into my leather Michael Kors mini crossbody. The
thought of that boisterous crowd spilling out into the hall
when Alex rings the bell makes my stomach lurch. Rat
might have been willing to run interference for me, but he
left an hour ago for Ever's house.

"Don't worry about it, honey." My dad can clearly read
my mind as he walks down the hall toward me, leaving
the living-room laughter behind. "Just have a good time
and be home before ten."

"Why can't we have one night at home without all these
guys hanging around?" I can't keep the frustration out of
my voice.

"You're not going to be home tonight anyway, so it
doesn't matter." My dad is always so rational. He pulls
me in for a hug. "You look fantastic."

"Thanks, Dad."

A tall African-American fireman named Leo saunters
into the hallway behind us, grinning at me. "Come on,
Linds. Let us meet the guy. We'll be nice. Promise."

As if on cue, the doorbell rings, and I look over at Dad
in a panic.

Save me.

Dad turns around and grabs the fireman by the shoulders. He pulls him back toward the living room. "Let's leave these two kids alone, Leo."

Finally. I take a deep breath and pull open the door.

Alex is standing on the front porch. He's wearing jeans and a striped navy-blue T-shirt. It looks like he got a haircut; his black hair is shorter than it was yesterday, and accentuates his sharp cheekbones and thick brows. My cheeks are suddenly hot.

Calm down, I tell myself. But I can't.

"Hi," I say as casually as I can muster.

"Is your house on fire?" Alex asks, motioning to the fire truck parked at the curb.

I step out on the porch and quickly shut the door behind me. "No." I laugh nervously. "It's just my mom's friends. I'll introduce you another time, okay?"

He nods and I step off the porch, eager to make a getaway before Fire Station Number 12 decides to get involved.

The coolness of the March night helps push away some of the first-date nerves.

I look down at Alex's feet. He's wearing a pair of navy Old Skool Vans.

When I glance back up to his face, he's looking at me and smiling. "Do I pass?"

Oh boy, do you. With flying colors!

"You look great," I say. His smile grows even wider and a hundred butterflies take flight in my stomach.

"You too," he says, then holds out his hand. I take it,

and he leads me down the sidewalk to the car parked at the curb.

Alex opens the passenger's side door and I get inside, smiling up at him as he shuts it behind me. I buckle my seat belt, roll down the window partway, and lean back against the leather seats of his older-model BMW. As Alex runs around the back of the car to get into the driver's side, I see Max standing out by his driveway and I lift a hand in greeting. He doesn't wave back.

"So where are we going?" I ask, once Alex starts up the car and pulls away from the curb. "What's the big surprise?"

Alex brakes for a red light. "I was thinking it would be fun to go bowling."

Are you kidding me? I was thinking soft music and a candlelit dinner or holding hands in a dark movie theater or something—*anything*—more romantic than BOWLING. I haven't bowled since I went to Max Rossi's eighth birthday party. I remember Max's mom thought it would be great if they gave a prize to the person with the lowest score, and I was the winner—or rather, loser in this case. The prize was a huge gold-colored medal I had to wear around my neck for the rest of the party that read "You Need Practice Award." Everyone thought it was hilarious. Except me. I stuffed that stupid medal in the back of my closet as soon as I got home that day and never set foot in a bowling alley again. I was horrible at bowling then and I'm sure nothing has changed since.

I glance over at Alex. He's smiling, so obviously proud of his decision, and I don't have the heart to tell him how horrible it sounds. I look out the side window to hide my expression.

"Great," I say, even though I don't really mean it. But I'm afraid of looking like a loser in front of Alex. Then my mother's voice whispers in my head. *Be fearless, Linden.* I close my eyes, count to three, and then open them slowly and take a deep breath.

Maybe I'll look silly, but I'm going to make the best of it. If Alex likes me, bad bowling isn't going to change his mind.

Ⓧ ♥ Ⓧ

The bowling alley smells like popcorn and feet. An eighties soundtrack cranks out above the noise of the pins falling and congratulatory yells.

The greasy-haired guy behind the counter's name tag says "Charlie." He asks me what size shoes I wear and reluctantly I tell him. When he pulls a pair off the shelf behind him and sprays the insides with some kind of disinfectant, I want to just turn and walk back out that front door. But I don't. Because right at that moment, Alex curls his arm around my waist and grins down at me like he's having the best time ever.

Charlie asks me, "Do you need socks?"

"No," I say, shaking my head. Thank God for the thick

boot socks I put on under my cowboy boots. I tell myself my feet won't actually touch the shoes.

"Do you need some help?" Alex asks, and I shake my head.

I remove my boots and carefully hand them to Charlie.

"This is going to be great," Alex says.

I'm still not so sure, but he's so happy not knowing the truth. And his arm feels so perfect around my waist. So I nod, picking up the ugly pink-and-black-striped shoes with two fingers, and head toward the racks of brightly colored bowling balls.

It takes a while to pick out just the right ball and get settled in at the lane. I choose a yellow ball with green swirls because I like the way it looks, but have no idea if it's the right size.

Alex gets everything set up at the scoring desk, typing his name first, then mine on the screen. Seeing *Linden* projected up there for everyone to look at makes me even more nervous.

A group of four ladies are at the lane next to us. They are all wearing coordinating striped shirts that say "Dolls with Balls" on the back in pink sparkle, and each has a bowling glove on one hand to match. Even their shoes are matching, and I'm jealous they don't have to share them with hundreds of other feet.

The tallest one, who's wearing retro eyeliner, smiles at me when I sit down. Her name, Belle, is embroidered over one pocket in bright pink. I nod at her self-consciously, then slide into the bright orange plastic chair next to Alex.

Alex goes first and knocks down most of the pins with the first roll. It looks effortless, his arm swinging gracefully at his side as he hurls the ball toward the pins at lightning speed. A baseball star *and* a bowling ace? Is there anything he can't do? And what in the world is he doing with a klutz like me?

His second ball knocks down the rest, and the Dolls with Balls high-five him and yell congratulations. Now it's my turn. All I can think of is how short the skirt of my dress is, and how everyone is looking at my backside. I take a couple of breaths to try to calm the frantic pounding in my head. Pointing the ugly shoes toward the pins, I swing my arm back as fast as I can, holding on tightly to the ball. Too late, I can feel it slipping away from my fingers. It sails out of my hand, flying through the air and bouncing across the floor toward the booth.

Crap.

I drop my head in embarrassment. I can feel the ghost of that stupid loser medal hanging there around my neck. Only now it's grown to the size of a bowling ball.

I turn around, clapping my hands over my mouth, to stare at Alex. He stands up, walks over to me, and slowly pulls my hands down from my face.

"Are you okay?" he asks. I nod, feeling the heat burning in my face. "How about some lessons?" he offers.

"That's probably a really good idea."

"Let's try this without the ball first. Face the pins."
Alex stands behind me, one hand sliding down my elbow
to my hand. My breath catches. "Swing your arm backward . . . like this." He pulls my hand gently back toward
his body, and suddenly bowling is the last thing on my
mind. His breath is in my hair. Against my neck. I look
over my shoulder, and he is so close I could almost kiss
him. But who does that at a bowling alley?

Then the moment is shattered.

"I really think you need a different ball." Belle is
standing beside the ball return with her hands on her
hips. "I can help you pick one out."

Reluctantly, I agree, and between her and Alex and the
rest of the Dolls, I eventually knock down a few pins and
avoid the gutter. Then something magical happens. All
the lights go off and everything glows—the balls . . . the
pins . . . Alex's teeth . . . my shirt. The Dolls with Balls
cheer and I can't help but smile, too.

I walk up to the line, glowing ball in hand, and throw
it out onto the lane. And to everyone's surprise, it rolls
straight and fast and right into the first pin. The chain reaction is impressive. I watch, mesmerized, as one pin after
another falls until the last one sways, then topples.

Oh my God.

My first strike!

I jump up and down, yelling and screaming like I've
just won a million dollars. The Dolls are whooping and
dancing around like they won, too. Then Alex sweeps me

up into his arms, congratulating me and hugging me so tight I forget all about the stupid worst-score medal from years ago.

I don't have to pretend anymore.

I *love* bowling, ugly shoes and all.

Later, we go to the tiny snack bar, and Alex picks up a plastic menu from the counter.

"May I take your order?" he asks, bowing slightly beside my chair. "Unfortunately, we have a bit of a limited menu tonight."

I pause, look down at the choices, then back up at him. "Is there a special you recommend?"

He winks at me. "I highly recommend the corn dogs."

"Perfect. Exactly what I had in mind."

"My kind of girl," he says, and we both blush. He heads over to order us the corn dogs and I watch him walk away, my head spinning from all the details. Like how his shirt bunches and tightens across the muscles of his back and the way his thick black hair curls up just a tiny bit right at the base of his neck. I swallow hard and look down at the tabletop.

When Alex comes back carrying the plates and drinks, we eat the corn dogs and share a plate of fries, laughing about my horrible start at bowling.

"Why didn't you tell me you couldn't bowl?" he asks, dipping a fry into a pool of catsup.

"Was it that obvious?"

He tilts his head and looks at me like I must be kidding.

I bite my bottom lip and then admit, "I didn't want you to think I didn't want to go with you."

"Did you want to go?" he asks, pausing with a French fry halfway to his mouth.

"No. I mean . . . " I look him in the eye. I don't want to lie to him. "I didn't want to go bowling, but I wanted to go with *you*."

His brows draw together. "I hope you still had fun."

"Absolutely," I say. "It was a blast."

"And you could have told me . . . " he says.

"I know. I'm working on the speaking-up thing. Sometimes I don't tell people what I'm thinking . . . but that's not your fault."

He hesitates and then says, "I like hearing what you think."

I freeze with the corn dog halfway to my mouth. The look on his face is sucking up all the oxygen in the room, but in a good way.

Then the door flies open and a group of middle school boys push into the tiny snack bar, slapping one another on the back and congratulating one another on a game well played. The moment between us is broken and we go back to casually eating French fries while the boys order soft drinks and hamburgers at the counter behind us.

Then Alex laughs and says, "If you hadn't come bowling, then we never would have seen how fast those Dolls could duck when that bowling ball was coming toward their heads."

I grin. "That was totally worth it."

I take another bite of the corn dog.

"What do you think of the food?" Alex asks.

"Your culinary tastes are excellent," I say.

"They should be. I've actually been working at one of my family's restaurants for . . . " He pauses. "Well, as long as I can remember. I've been a cook, waiter, dishwasher, and busboy. You name it, I've done it."

"How many restaurants does your family own?" I ask, tucking my hair behind my ear. I fumble for the straw in front of me and lean in to take a long sip of Coke, my gaze never leaving his face.

"The new one out on Highway 30 will be our third when it opens up next month. I'll help out there when baseball season is over," he says.

I wonder how it would feel to walk through the door and see Alex waiting tables. I bet he's good at it. Just like he's good at baseball and bowling. And hugging. Instantly, the heat is back and crawling up my throat to my face. The snack bar smells like hamburgers and French fries, but all I can think of is the clean, soapy smell of Alex's neck.

"How is your story coming along?" he asks me, and I blink at the reality jolt.

I make a face and sigh. "Not great. I don't really have an idea."

"I'm sure it's hard," Alex says. "I think it's amazing how stories and characters can just come out of your brain," he says, and takes another bite of his corn dog. The boys at the counter take their food to go and head back out to the sound of crashing pins and shouts of celebration. The door closes behind them, shutting out the noise and leaving only a faint whiff of hamburgers behind.

"It gets a little crowded in there sometimes," I say, tapping my forehead with my finger.

He raises his eyebrows in question.

"I'm always making up some kind of backstory," I tell him. "Like that guy working behind the counter?"

Alex nods and looks over.

"See his silver metallic computer case by the cash register?"

Alex nods again. "I do now."

"Pretty out of place for a guy working in a bowling alley snack bar, don't you think?" I ask, but then lean across the table and quickly add, "So I'm thinking he actually works for the CIA and he's carrying around classified documents inside."

Alex laughs but looks impressed. "See. I told you that brain of yours was incredibly cool. I never notice those things, and I sure wouldn't have thought of anything like that even if I did."

I hesitate. I've never tried to explain my writing brain to anyone before, but his attitude makes this part of me feel special and unique—not totally bonkers.

"It's not only about the thinking part. It's also about putting it into words, and that's the part I'm struggling with right now." I lean back into my chair, pushing away from the table. "Do you know how many writers have tried to describe the green of the grass or the blue of the sky? Hundreds? Thousands? I have to somehow come up with something different. Different words in a different order. Something better?"

"That's a lot of pressure to put on yourself." He finishes the last bite of the corn dog and wipes the crumbs off his mouth with the paper towel.

"Even more if you consider the reader is a totally unknown partner in this whole thing. Say I wrote a story about a cow and two people read it. One person may never have seen a cow, and the other may have lived on a farm with cows all their life."

"Never thought about it like that before, but you can't predict what someone is going to think before you even write it." He dips the tip of the empty corn dog stick in the edge of the catsup and draws out a red line on the paper plate. "I guess that makes it hard. Risky."

I nod. "And I'm not a fan of risk-taking."

"I don't know much about writing, but I do know base-ball, and a good coach always helps. Maybe you need some-one to read your stuff and give you feedback. Like a coach."

It is good advice, but I'm not sure I'm ready. Just talking to Alex about writing is a huge step for me. And even though he's making me feel like a rock star right now, I don't know if I can trust him, or anyone else, to actually read my writing.

"It's hard for me to share my stories with anyone," I admit. "If someone reads what I write, then they know how I think. Who I am," I say. "They might not like me . . . I mean, the story."

"But if someone never reads what you write, are you really a writer?" he asks.

I frown, thinking about it. "What came first—the chicken or the egg?"

"Exactly. Can you be a real writer if no one actually reads what you write?"

I don't like his logic. Mainly because it's hitting way too close to the truth. I let out a fake little laugh. "Sure you can. Anyone can write."

This time I'm glad when our conversation is interrupted. A man wearing a black T-shirt and jeans comes through the door. His reading glasses are propped up on top of his head and he has bands around his ankles, the kind that keep pant legs out of bike spokes. The man pulls his glasses off his head and reads the menu, then orders a latte from the guy behind the counter.

Alex nods in the direction of the two men, then leans across the table. "You think he's the contact?"

I blink at him, not understanding at first. Then I get it and smile slowly. Not only is Alex supporting my wild imagination, he's actually joining in. "Yeah," I say. "He's passing him the secret code on that napkin right about . . . now."

We both watch the man settle into a seat by the window. He blows on his cup of coffee, then stretches his legs out onto the seat in front of him. When he glances over to see us watching, we simultaneously look down at the table.

"The napkin," Alex whispers, rolling his eyes toward the man at the window. "He just crumpled it up and put it in his pocket."

After we finish laughing at the close call, Alex says, "Name me one person who wrote something that was never read."

I don't want to hear this. It's making way too much sense. "I can't . . . because I don't know who they are."

"My point exactly." Alex is staring at me so hard I have to look away.

"Okay. I do want people to read what I write, but what if they don't accept me?" Then I blurt out, "Or, even worse, what if they accept me and I'm not good enough to actually keep going? What if I let everyone down?"

"What if you let yourself down? What if you don't even try?"

It is a huge dilemma. One I've struggled with in my head for a long time.

"I'm scared," I say quietly. "What if they don't like it?"

"What if they do?" he asks. Then he smiles in a way that makes my neck go hot.

(X) (♥) (X)

When we leave the bowling alley, Alex drives me home. As he turns onto my street, he says, "I have a baseball game in Conroe on Monday, but I was wondering if you want to come over to my house Tuesday after school and do homework?"

My heart jumps. I'll get to see where Alex lives. "That sounds great," I say, not even bothering to hide my big grin. "I can ride the bus to school and then ride home with you?"

He nods, pulling the car up to the curb. "But I have to warn you, my family is pretty crazy right now."

I laugh. "Crazier than a house full of firefighters?"

He grimaces. "You haven't met my grandmother yet."

"Does she live with you?"

"No, she lives with my uncle and my cousin Luis. But these days she's always at our house helping with the quinceañera plans."

"Your uncle owns the Rivera Funeral Home, right?"

He nods, then turns off the car. It has been a perfect evening, and I don't want this date to end. Not by a long shot. But he opens his door and reluctantly I get out, too. I lead the way up the sidewalk.

"Wait," he says quietly behind me before I can reach the front steps.

I look back over my shoulder and his hand is reaching out for mine. I turn around and take his hand.

"You don't have to go in yet, do you? Let's sit out here a minute."

My fingers tangle into his. I look around at my front yard. "Where?"

"Here." He sinks onto the grass and gently pulls me down beside him. It should probably feel weird to be sitting outside on my front lawn on a Saturday night, but it doesn't. Instead, I almost forget where we are and that the romantic lighting is really just the streetlight two doors down.

We sit like that a few minutes, legs outstretched. A car rumbles down the street in front of us, the headlights briefly lighting up the "Vote Max Rossi for Student Council President" sign on the lawn across the street, but then it is quiet again. The sky is black now, clouds covering all the stars above. A half-moon slides into view briefly and is quickly swallowed up again by the darkness. It reminds me of something I haven't thought about for a very long time.

"I was fascinated by stars when I was a kid," I say, leaning back on my elbows. "When we used to go camping, and there were no city lights, I would stare up at the stars for hours."

"Was this before or after the s'mores?"

I'm surprised he remembered. "After. There would be one or two stars out at first, then by the time the fire died down to just the glowing embers, there would be layers upon layers. Deeper and deeper. It was like you could almost see into another universe."

"That would be a great beginning to one of your stories," he says. "Sorry we can't see any stars tonight."

"There's nothing to apologize for," I whisper. "It's good just the way it is."

Then we sit there for a long time in the quiet because it's perfectly okay to not say anything at all. The air is so still, I can feel his body moving gently beside me as he breathes.

Finally, Alex speaks. "If you could choose to be a character in any book, who would you be?"

"I'm more of a secondary kind of character," I say. "Like the best friend."

"But if you *were* the main character?" he asks.

"I don't know," I say, thinking about it for a minute. "There are so many to choose from and they are all so different. Jo from *Little Women*. Anne from *Anne of Green Gables*. Katniss from *The Hunger Games*. I could go on and on."

"Why haven't you recommended any of those books to me?"

It's a good question, and I think about it for a minute. "I didn't know if you would like them. They're about girls."

I can see him smile even in the dark. "I like girls."

"I'm a girl," I say.

He laughs quietly. "I know."

He raises his hand, still caught up in mine, and traces his thumb gently against my lips. My face explodes with heat, and when his hand slips away, I lean in toward him. The first kiss is soft. Just a touch. There is one more and then another, longer and deeper. I slide my hands up his arm to his shoulders. I wrap my arms around his neck, feeling the power of his muscles under my hands. He leans back on the grass, pulling me against his chest, and we are kissing . . .

And kissing.

And kissing.

Ross Adams & Raylene Anderson

IS SHE WORTHY?

Here's what you are saying:

* Talk about an odd couple. He's six inches shorter and ten times smarter.

* No way this is going to last!

* He must have a thing for crazy girls.

* She's absolutely worthy! She's sweet and a kind-hearted friend.

* She's just a joke. Nobody can be serious about her.

CHAPTER EIGHT

On Monday, everything looks the same, but things are definitely *not* the same, because this is the first day of school after I kissed Alex Rivera in my front yard and it's all I've been thinking about since.

When I get to my locker, Alex is waiting for me there, and my heart leaps. So Saturday night wasn't a dream. It was real.

"Hey," he says, coming over to take my hand, which sets off a quivery feeling in my stomach. "Saturday was great."

I nod. "It really was." Kids are walking all around us. A few heads are turning, noticing that Alex Rivera and I are standing together by my locker. That clearly means something. For once, I don't care, though. All I can think about is how much I want to kiss him again.

"I have to catch the bus after fourth period to go to the baseball game today," Alex says, "but we're still on for my house tomorrow?"

I nod. Then I see Nikki coming down the hall behind Alex. She raises her brows sky high and mouths the words, "We need to talk."

She texted me on Sunday asking about the date and wanting all the details, but I wasn't ready to talk about it yet, so I just answered that it went great. An obvious understatement. I know we'll catch up more later.

The bell rings then, and Alex surprises me by leaning forward and kissing me right on the mouth. In school!

I jerk backward because I'm not expecting it and it ends up a totally awkward kind of face bump.

"Sorry," I mumble, running a hand across my mouth nervously and looking around to see who is watching. I'm not so sure public displays of affection are my thing.

"Sorry," Alex says back, laughing nervously. I'm glad we can be awkward together

"See you," Alex says, waving at me and heading for the science wing. I wave back and start walking toward English class. It's funny to think that we weren't awkward at all when we were kissing on Saturday night. I blush and smile at the memory.

$$ \text{(x)} \ \text{(♥)} \ \text{(x)} $$

At lunchtime, I get to the cafeteria early, so I sit down on an empty bench to wait for Nikki. I take out my phone. I have time to post a few prom dress photos and upload some promposal videos to the Hornet. I get most of them from other people's posts, but some have been emailed directly to me now that the word is getting around that I'm handling publicity.

So far, food is a major theme. Ethan Hudson brought a

box of Shipley doughnuts to volleyball practice with "Please doughnut say no" spelled out in icing on top. Another guy held up a six pack of Mountain Dew with a sign that read "Dew you want to go to prom with me?" And my personal favorite so far was Sophia Murray, who sent her boyfriend, Aiden, a Domino's pizza in homeroom with "Prom?" spelled out in pepperoni. I'm beginning to feel a little obsessed with the whole thing, and I haven't written a single word of my story for the contest.

I close out of the Hornet and click over to Worthy. It's become a habit. Not necessarily a good one. It's like this app has focused everyone's opinions through the lens of a magnifying glass. It's lit the student body on fire. We're all happily judging away.

The comments about Raylene and Ross are not just on the app anymore. Facebook posts, tweets, stories on Snapchat, even some sneaked Instagram photos of the latest nominee try to argue some point—she's too tall, too dumb, too poor, too something. And I can hear people talking in the halls, too. Opinions and whispers everywhere.

Still no one knows who is behind the curtain. Who is pulling the strings.

I glance up to see Nikki coming down the hall toward me, so I close out of the app and stand up. My best friend grins eagerly, and I know it's time to spill the beans.

"So after this big, romantic kissing scene, do you think Alex will ask you to the prom?" Nikki asks me as we sit at our table, our food barely touched because we were so busy catching up.

I glance around. The windows and walls of the cafeteria are covered in signs reminding everyone of the upcoming prom. The one scrawled on the window across from where Nikki and I always sit reads, "Some enchanted evening, when you find your true love . . . AT PROM."

Last week, I sat in this same place, looked at that sign, and thought, *Not if you don't go.*

But everything has changed and the possibilities are tantalizing. Maybe I *will* be going to the prom. With Alex. I feel like twirling around the cafeteria with my arms outstretched like some kind of musical theater star.

Beyond the graffiti on the windows it is a drizzly, wet day. Standing puddles of water under the cloudy skies made running for shelter more like dodging. The weather is in direct contrast to my mood. I see Kat over against the windows talking to her friends. She looks up and our eyes meet. She nods at me; the corner of her mouth turning up into a smile. We only talk at the library. It is like some unwritten rule. At school, we just nod at each other in passing or across the cafeteria crowds. I'm not sure why.

"We've only gone on one date," I say to Nikki, looking back down at my peanut butter sandwich. I try to play it cool. "We'll see."

"Yeah, yeah," Nikki says. She sees right through me. "So where is he?"

"During the baseball season, he usually spends lunch period in the weight room with the other players. And there's an away game this afternoon in Conroe, so . . . " My voice drops off and I shrug. I know way more about Alex's activities than I realized.

Nikki squints her eyes at me. "When are you going out again?"

"I'm going over to his house after school tomorrow, but that's not really a date. We're going to study together."

Maybe he'll ask me to prom then. Now Nikki has me thinking about such things, and I don't want to get my hopes up.

I change the subject, picking up my phone. "Did you know the Mayfair filter is the best one to use on Instagram to get more followers?"

"Says who?"

"A Fortune 500 report I found online. There's a whole science to this social media thing."

Nikki doesn't seem impressed, so I continue to share my newly gained information. "The best day for posts is Sunday because statistically the fewest images are posted on that day. So your image gets the most visibility."

"You're totally making this stuff up." Nikki sighs.

"No. I swear. I've been researching it."

"Aren't you supposed to be researching World War II for world history?"

"This is more interesting," I say.

"True." Nikki stuffs her half-eaten sandwich back into the Ziploc bag in front of her.

"And it seems to be working so far," I say. "If people aren't talking about Worthy, they're talking about prom."

"Have you seen those comments about Raylene?" Nikki frowns and I nod, sighing. "Nobody deserves that kind of judgment. Usually people just say that stuff behind your back; now it's right there on the screen for everyone to read." Nikki glances at me, her eyebrows furrowed. "You voted, didn't you?" she asks me.

"Yeah," I whisper. "Did you?"

Nikki nods slowly, then she shrugs. "Yeah. I guess we're all guilty."

Nikki takes an apple out of her Rebecca Minkoff Micro backpack. She puts on her "Futuristic Kitty" exaggerated cat-eye sunglasses and takes a carefully posed selfie of herself taking a big bite of the apple.

"What are you doing?" I ask.

"Sending this picture to Jake to show him how healthy I'm eating."

I'm a good friend. But I don't want to hear Nikki talk about Jake. Especially when it is always about her changing for him.

If I were my mother, I would say, "Don't let a guy bring you down because of his own insecurities" or something profound like that. Instead, I say, "That's weird."

"Why?" She takes another bite of her apple.

"You're the one who always says size doesn't matter." I pick up a napkin and wipe the last crumbs of my sandwich off the edge of my mouth.

"Who said this was about size? Besides, what's wrong with wanting to eat healthier?"

"Nothing. If you are doing it for yourself."

She holds up her phone and does another couple of poses. "Of course I'm doing it for me. Who else?"

"Did you know more people die by taking selfies than from shark attacks?" I ask, but she just takes off the sunglasses and rolls her eyes at me, tapping away at her phone. I catch a snippet of a conversation from three girls walking in front of the table carrying cafeteria trays.

"Maybe he has self-esteem issues. I said he can definitely do better," the first one says. "I'm saying no. I never thought they went together. She's way too silly for him."

"I don't know. I think they're cute together. I say yes. Worthy," says the taller one, dramatically.

"He's a Pisces. She's a Leo. Not a good match. I vote no," says the other, over her shoulder.

"Have you even looked at the comments? She's totally going to make it," says the second girl as they walk out of my hearing and to a table over by the windows.

I pull out my phone and check on my newly created hashtag, #hornetsprom. My recent tweet—*Get expert tips everyday on prom fashions by following @hornetpage on Twitter*—is getting quite a few favorites and retweets. I follow back every single one because, if there is one thing I've learned from all my research, that's important. It's the personal touch that matters.

Nikki frowns across the table at me. "What are you doing?"

"I have to follow up with every person who tweeted or posted to the Hornet. It doesn't matter whether it's good, bad, or neutral. I need to respond. Ignoring feedback is leaving fans behind."

"You're really getting obsessed with this," Nikki says.

"It's a lot of work." I heart the last Instagram photo and look up from my phone. "But it feels creative."

Nikki nods, taking another bite of her apple and chewing slowly. "And you're getting tons of ideas for your story, right?"

I don't say anything.

"Right?"

"Absolutely." I'm lying and she knows it. I haven't written a single word since I started the publicity campaign. This new obsession has become my go-to procrastination destination.

We both look over to the popular table, where Taylor is sitting with Heather Middleton and a petite blonde cheerleader named Mia Rogers.

"Since when did Heather get to join the Lovelies?" Nikki asks.

I twist off the top of my water bottle and take a drink

before answering. "Her father has a limo company. She's getting a lot of new friends these days."

Wolfgang Gines, a senior football player, is at the table. And he's all cozied up to Taylor like he's moved right into Liam's empty spot. Max is there, too, but on the other end, sitting next to Jayla. It's like opposing football teams that just took the field for the coin toss. They are all making nice, but everyone knows the prom queen smackdown is brewing and everyone is picking a side—Team Taylor or Team Jayla.

"The word is Taylor's got the best chance, because of her being on Worthy and all. Free publicity," Nikki says.

I make a face. "That reminds me. I need to talk to Taylor about the prom publicity."

"Ugh. Good luck with that." Nikki pulls down the sunglasses and peers at me over the top.

"You're the one who got me into all this in the first place," I say, whining a little.

"If you didn't want to do it, you should have spoken up," Nikki says, and I'm mentally kicking myself because I know she's right.

I swallow hard, then mumble, "I'll talk to her later."

Nikki smirks at me. "Why don't you go over there right now?" She's daring me. The same way she dared me to jump out of Max's treehouse when we were seven.

I broke my arm.

I lock eyes with Nikki and stand up, taking the dare.

This is probably going to turn out just as bad as the tree house incident, but I'm doing it anyway. I try to focus on steadying my heart rate, then start the long trek across the tiled floor.

There's a reason why I'm a follower. I'm good at it. Without someone leading the way, the casual stroll across the cafeteria seems to take forever. I stand beside the table, waiting and trying not to run back to Nikki. I figure it's cooler to stand here and not say anything than to try to yell over the conversations to get everyone's attention. So I wait, shifting from one Sophia Webster butterfly flat to the other. It takes a couple of minutes for anyone to even look my direction, but the longer I wait for someone to notice, the more nervous I get. One of the *Teen Vogue* articles I read recently said you should fake fitting in until you believe it yourself. I reposition my feet for the best possible angle and try not to look terrified. I'm definitely faking it.

Taylor finally looks up when Heather shoves an elbow in her side and makes eyes at me. Wolfgang has one arm draped across her shoulders. He looks at me. "What's your name?"

I open my mouth to answer, but Taylor says, "Her name is Linden. She's the one I told you about."

I'm the topic of conversation between Taylor and Wolfgang? Is that a good thing?

He stares at me, but all I can do is shrug.

"She's our publicity chair," Taylor announces, surprising

me with her enthusiasm. The talking stops. Taylor pats the empty spot beside her. "Sit down. Join us."

I glance back over my shoulder to see Nikki staring at me with raised eyebrows. I shrug and slide onto the bench beside Taylor. Mia flashes me a fake, I'm-only-tolerating-you-because-she-invited-you smile.

"That's what I wanted to talk to you about," I say, then look down the table at Max and Jayla. I quickly add, "All of you."

"What?" Max asks from the end of the table.

"I've been doing some research on internet marketing and thought it'd be a good idea to have a contest. Maybe give away a couple of tickets to the prom for retweets and tags?"

Jayla nods with an accompanying rattle of silver jewelry. She's wearing a wide-legged striped jumpsuit, her hair in a chic braided bun. "Might be a good idea. I just checked, and we're close to breaking the record for ticket sales."

"Fantastic," I say. "If we have all these followers in place before the prom, just imagine how many people will see the photos of the actual night."

I can almost see the hamsters in Taylor's brain running around that tiny wheel while she thinks that over. "So photos of the prom queen"—she looks around the table—"and her court . . . would be everywhere."

"Practically viral," I say.

"They are going to announce the election results at the dance," Max says. "It wouldn't hurt to see the future student council president rocking out on the dance floor. That's what we politicians are supposed to do, right? Shake hands and kiss babes?"

He looks around the table, but no one laughs at his lame joke.

Our publicity is your publicity. It should be my motto.

"It's brilliant," Taylor says, and her groupies nod in agreement. "I'll totally help."

The bell rings then, and everyone scatters. I stand up to go and end up walking out of the cafeteria with Jayla, Taylor, and Mia. It feels strange but not terrible.

Jayla is scrolling on her phone. "So who do you think is behind Worthy?" she asks as we walk down the hall.

Taylor glances around. "I don't know. Some guy who's like a tech genius."

"Who says it's a guy?" Mia asks. "Girls can be way worse at this judgment thing."

I fiddle with my own phone. *You think?*

"And girls can be tech geniuses," I point out testily.

"You're right. It could even be someone we know." Taylor lowers her voice.

"Yeah. It could be anybody," I say.

It could even be you, Taylor.

IS RAYLENE WORTHY?

The votes are in . . .

Stay tuned . . .

CHAPTER NINE

It's been a long time since I've had to ride the bus to school in the morning. But since I'm catching a ride home with Alex this afternoon, I stand outside on the sidewalk and wait for it to arrive. There's a screech of brakes when the bus rounds the corner, then it rumbles to a stop in front of me. The doors swish open and I climb up the steps behind Max Rossi. Most of the seats are empty. I pass two girls talking to each other and one freshman boy on the other side. He watches me as I pass, smiling hopefully, but I keep going. The bus starts moving and I'm thrown into an empty seat right next to Max.

I try to slide as far away from him as possible, but just then the bus rounds a corner and throws me into his side. I push myself back upright and glare at him. Max just grins, pulling his backpack out of the way.

"Welcome to the world of the unwashed," he says.

"What are you doing on the bus, anyway? Grounded?" I ask.

"I'm not above supporting public transportation," Max

says. "Besides, it's a great opportunity to get to know my constituents."

He leans over the seat in front of us and hands a button to a freshman kid, clapping him on the shoulder. It says, "Vote for Max. Senior class president." The boy takes it and pins it to his T-shirt with a smile, obviously flattered by the attention.

Max holds another one out to me. "Here you go."

I shake my head. "Doesn't go with my outfit."

He shrugs and slides the pin back in his backpack. "So how's your love life?"

"Fine." It's none of his business.

My phone buzzes. It's Alex, texting that he'll pick me up after school to go over to his house to study. I exit out of my messages, smiling down at the phone.

Max gives a dramatic sigh and puts one hand on my shoulder. "Looks like you are falling hard for a certain someone. Am I right?"

"Why do you say that?" I shrug off his hand. It's always good to answer a question with a question. It buys some time to try to think of the right answer.

"I saw you guys standing by your locker yesterday. You got all soft and mushy in your face."

I want to deny it, but I can't. I do like Alex. A lot. I like his thick black hair and his eyes that are only a shade lighter. I like the way his forehead wrinkles into a deep line between his eyebrows when he's listening really hard. I like his power and grace on the baseball field.

Actually, there isn't anything I can think of that I don't like about Alex.

My phone buzzes again and I glance down, thinking it might be Alex again. Instead it's a notification from Worthy that says Raylene's results will be posted this afternoon. Max looks over my shoulder to read the screen. I try to block the view by turning my back to him.

"Nobody was surprised that Taylor was worthy of Liam, but Raylene and Ross are a bit of a wild card." He looks over at me. "Don't you think?"

It's something I've been thinking about, too, but I bury my nose in my phone and try to tune him out. The comments about Raylene make me shudder.

"Oh, don't act all holier than thou. If you think about it, it's really a community service," Max says. "Everyone has an opinion and this app is just letting them share freely. Not in whispers behind backs, but right out in the open."

I look up from my phone. Max is looking out the window, not at me. "I don't care about Worthy," I tell him, but I know that isn't completely true. I've been voting right along with everyone else. Guilt pokes at my insides.

Max keeps talking. "Remember that card game we used to play when we were kids? Concentration? You had to turn the cards over and find a match. It's the same way with relationships. When you turn over the cards and look, you just know."

His attitude makes me angry. "It's not just about looks.

Besides, we're all the same inside. Same skeleton. Same lungs."

"Yeah, right," Max says. "You tell that to Taylor. Go tell her that you're exactly the same as her. See how far that gets you into the popular crowd."

"I don't want to be part of Taylor's crowd."

Max looks at me like he doesn't believe me. To be honest, I don't believe me.

Ⓧ ♥ Ⓧ

The bus pulls up in the circular drive and screeches to a halt. The doors open and the kids at the front start getting off. After I step out onto the sidewalk, I head to a bench to wait for Nikki. With a quick wave over his shoulder, Max keeps going toward the front doors, passing out his campaign buttons along the way.

I watch the crowd and wait, hoping Nikki is going to be on time for once in her life. All through the parking lot, people trudge between cars and across the grass toward the big brick building in front of them.

My writing brain kicks into gear and I welcome the distraction. Two girls are standing by the flagpole. One wears bright yellow rain boots and holds a pink-and-gray-striped umbrella. The other one, shorter, with dark, frizzy hair, takes a picture as the first girl holds the umbrella in front of her body and twirls it. They trade the umbrella and take turns snapping more pictures. I don't know them, which makes creating the story even easier. I tilt my head, thinking, and it comes to me in a minute.

The frizzy-haired one's father has just been transferred to Dubai. She wants to remember the Texas rain and her best friend because all she knows about Dubai is that it is in the desert. Her father's office will be on the 138th floor of the Burj Khalifa, the tallest building in the world, and they will live in an apartment nearby. She doesn't want to go.

I watch as the two girls with the umbrella hug, then walk off in opposite directions, both looking down at their phones.

A guy walks up wearing faded, light blue jeans and well-worn cowboy boots, a phone to his ear. His jeans are long, wet, and frayed at the hem, and his brown hoodie is pulled up over the top of his camouflage baseball cap. I decide he is talking to his mother about her latest doctor's report. It doesn't look good and he's going to have to take more responsibility out at the ranch.

But then my mental storytelling is interrupted by the voices behind me.

Over by the trash cans, two kids huddle over their phones, discussing Worthy.

"Are you kidding? Give me that phone . . . " A tall boy with shaggy blond hair grabs at the phone of the girl sitting next to him. She pulls her phone away, laughing.

"She's just too tall for him," she says. "That's why I voted no."

I groan, dropping my head into my hands. I want to stand up and scream at them all to shut up. When I look up again, I see Torrey Grey walking between two cars. She stops to dig around in her oversized purse, then pulls out a mirror and lip gloss. Holding the mirror in one hand, she carefully applies the lip gloss, then smiles at her reflection.

Raylene gets out of a car two rows back. "Wait for me!" she yells.

"Run!" Torrey yells back at her. "I'm not getting another tardy because of you."

Ross and a couple of other football players are hanging out by the front doors watching as the girls run across the parking lot. They are laughing and talking so loudly everyone can hear them.

"Here comes your girlfriend, Ross," Wolfgang Gines says. "Have you heard the latest blonde joke?"

Ross frowns and doesn't say anything.

Wolf leans into his face. "What do you call a smart blonde? A golden retriever."

Wolf punches Ross in the shoulder and Liam laughs hysterically. "I got one. I got one. How do you make a blonde's eyes light up?"

He waits a beat, then says, "Shine a flashlight in her ear."

I want to stand up and walk over to them. To make them stop. But I know how quickly their attention can turn to someone else, and I can't bring myself to get up off the bench. I swallow hard.

Wolf turns and says to the other guys, "I guess Ross is not exactly looking for brains."

Ross pushes him away and kind of fake punches him in one arm. The book in Wolf's hand goes flying to the ground. He grabs on to Ross's shirt and pushes him back against the metal trash cans. The sound is loud enough to cause heads to turn, but when they see it is Wolf wrestling with some kid, they just go back to their morning conversations.

I am sure Ross is dead, but then Wolf laughs.

"Yeah, you're crazy about her," he says, leaning into Ross's face and making his brown eyes go wide for emphasis.

"Shut up." Ross forces the words through his clenched teeth. The other guys laugh loudly and slap him on the back. And right at that moment, Raylene rushes up to give Ross a big hug.

"Hi, babe," she says, and gives him a kiss right on the mouth, completely oblivious to the rest of the group. Ross stands there with a totally outraged look on his face, but I can't tell if he's mad at Wolf or at Raylene.

After third period, I open my locker door and stare inside at the stack of books and notebooks. I glance to the side and see Raylene and Ross standing over by the trophy case. Just like everyone else, I can't help but stare. Ross cocks his head to one side, looking into Raylene's face and stroking her arm. He asks her something and she nods but doesn't look happy. Her head falls forward, her hair in her face, and he reaches out to brush it back. She looks up at him and gives him a shaky smile. I look away, embarrassed by the intimacy of the moment. The look on Raylene's face makes my stomach hurt.

"I hear there are some kids starting a betting pool for Raylene. The odds are pretty much fifty-fifty right now." Kat Lee is standing beside my locker, leaning against the wall and breaking the no-talking-at-school rule. She's wearing ripped jeans, a black T-shirt, and a smirk on her bright red lips. "What do you think? Is she worthy or not?"

"Why are you asking me?" I ask, pulling out my math book and slamming my locker door with way more force than it needs.

"Because you're just as bad as the rest of them."

"I didn't write any of those comments," I say.

"You don't post those horrible comments, you just vote." Kat's voice is bitter. "You're right. That's not at all the same. It's not nearly so bad."

Color burns up my neck, but I don't say anything.

Kat shakes her head. "What? You seem to be enjoying this Worthy drama just like everyone else."

She's right. Finally, I say, "Raylene doesn't deserve this."

Kat narrows her eyes at me. "Who knows? Maybe you're the one behind it."

I shake my head. "You know that isn't true."

"I'm not sure I know anything about you anymore." She turns and starts to walk away. "Anyway, it's too late. It has a life of its own now. You can't stop it."

CHAPTER TEN

In Spanish class that afternoon, Taylor walks down the aisle and smiles in my direction. I know she's trying to kiss up to me, but I'm not fooled. Once prom is over and she's crowned junior prom queen, she won't give me the time of day. At least I'll have the satisfaction of inventing an amazing publicity campaign. I know my creative energy should be focused on the story contest, but now that I've started the prom publicity, I just can't quit.

Taylor slides into the seat beside me, mainly because it is empty.

Mrs. Boggs, the Spanish teacher, is late as usual. The rumor is she never wears the same dress twice in one school year. Since it's well past midyear, the suspense is building, and as far as anyone can remember, the rumor is holding up to the scrutiny of all the girls in fourth period.

It's not her outfits that get my attention. I'm more interested in the story behind the framed photo on her desk. I saw it last week when I went up to ask about the homework assignment. In it, Mrs. Boggs is standing in front of a grave holding a bouquet of purple hydrangeas, and even though Ray-Ban sunglasses cover her eyes, she looks like she's crying. Which makes sense because she's at a cemetery and all, but then I notice more. The tombstone has cat statues on top of it and is engraved with the name "Rattenborg." I wonder who is buried there and what the connection is to Mrs. Boggs, but it seems rude to ask.

"I might have seen that blue dress she wore last Wednesday before," Mia is saying to Jayla. She keeps fiddling with the tiny silver megaphone around her neck just to remind everybody that she's a cheerleader. *Like we could forget.*

Mrs. Boggs's Spanish class is considered one of the easier electives, and it meets the foreign language requirement for graduation, so all the Lovelies are here.

Raylene is in this class, too. I watch her across the room. She's sitting stock still at her desk, her phone clutched in her hand, her eyes glued to the screen. She looks pale. She must be waiting for the results to come in. Ugh. I can't imagine that feeling.

"No, absolutely not," Heather says. "I write a description of every single dress each period and draw a picture. I have it right here." Heather reaches into her backpack and waves a pink-striped spiral notebook at Mia. Leave it to Heather to have meticulously recorded each outfit. She has probably written down what everyone ate for lunch, too.

"You'd do a lot better at Spanish if you took notes like Heather," Taylor tells Mia. Then she and Mia laugh like that's the funniest thing in the universe because nobody wants to be like Heather.

As usual, Heather is oblivious. "I could tutor you after school," she tells Mia, and that just makes them laugh even more.

I listen to the conversation but don't join in. All semester, I watched them trade boyfriends, start fights, end fights, and mostly critique everything—clothes, speech, hair, earrings, shoes, even fingernails. So including teachers in their critical conversations is no surprise.

When Mrs. Boggs finally does come in, five minutes after the tardy bell rings, she's wearing a blue flowered dress that no one can remember seeing before. Rushing over to her desk, she plops down an overstuffed satchel, then asks Heather Middleton to call the roll. Not surprisingly, Heather is sitting in the front row just waiting for that kind of assignment.

"Did you finish that reading?" Taylor leans across the aisle to ask Raylene, who is trying to hide her phone under the desk so Mrs. Boggs can't see it. I don't think Taylor really cares what the response is, because she doesn't wait for an answer. "I didn't even get the first page read before I fell asleep. BORING."

"Probably because you were tired from going to the movies," Raylene says, still looking down at her phone.

Taylor glares at her. "How did you know I was at the movies last night?"

"You checked in. I'm your friend, remember?"

Some friend, I think, remembering how Taylor voted *no* on Worthy.

"Oh yeah. I forgot." Taylor laughs, then reaches into her pocket for some lip gloss. She slathers the pink shiny stuff all over her mouth and then says, "Facebook is so done anyway. Instagram and Snapchat are so much better. I'm definitely going to have more Instagram followers than Jayla by the end of next month."

"Congrats," I say.

For some reason this turns her focus to me. "So what's your new big idea? The promposal videos are cute, but all the same. We need something original."

Now she's the expert on internet marketing?

"I have some things in the works," I say. Taylor's eyebrows rise and she waits. She knows I'm bluffing.

"Like what?"

"Well . . . " My voice trails off and I glance down at the floor to think for a minute. Taylor is wearing a pair of Steve Madden boots that I've always admired, and my brain grasps at straws. "Shoes," I say.

"What about them?" Mia asks, her eyes narrowing. She taps her tiny kitten heels on the tile floor.

"You're right, Taylor," I say. "We need something totally different, but still fun. Prom dresses are overdone. Besides, no one wants to show their dress to everyone before the big night."

"Duh," says Mia.

But I'm just warming up, and the idea is really starting

to take shape. "So . . . I'm thinking selfie shots of potential prom shoes. We can tag them . . ." My voice trails off.

"Fab footwear!" Mia chimes in.

"Sensational slippers," Raylene says, her eyes focused on her phone under the desk. "Goes along with the Enchanted Evening theme."

"Perfect," I say. "We can give out a gift certificate to the shoe store downtown to the pic with the most likes."

Mrs. Boggs is, as usual, oblivious to our talking as she begins the Spanish lesson.

Taylor taps her fingers against the top of her desk with her pale pink polished nails, her blue eyes gazing up to the ceiling. We all wait. Finally, she says, "I like it."

It feels like high praise and that I deserve it.

Then Taylor says, "You can announce the winners at the dance. Right before the court is named."

And just like that, my mental celebration is cut short. Nobody except Nikki knows I don't have a date to prom yet. "Maybe," I say.

"No maybes," Taylor says. "You've worked hard on this publicity thing and deserve to share the spotlight."

Mia nods in agreement. "Absolutely."

Nikki shrugs and I shoot her a look. We'll talk about this later.

Suddenly, I hear Raylene's phone ping with an update.

Everyone looks over at her. I watch as Raylene's face turns even paler. Abruptly, she stands up and walks over to Mrs. Boggs's desk. "Can I go to the bathroom?" she asks, holding her stomach for emphasis. "I'm not feeling so well."

Instantly, Taylor grabs her phone out of her bag. She smiles down at the screen and shakes her head. "Poor thing," she whispers.

My own stomach drops. Just like that, without having to look at my phone, I know.

So sorry, Raylene!

63% say NO!

You are NOT WORTHY!

Maybe Ross should rethink his choices?
Just saying . . .

CHAPTER ELEVEN

I'm still thinking about Raylene and Worthy as Alex drives me to his house after school. How must Raylene have felt when she saw the negative verdict? I almost want to bring it up with Alex, but then he says, "We're almost there." I feel a jolt of nerves and forget about everything else. I take in my surroundings outside of the car window.

I'm a little surprised at the size of the houses on Alex's street. I figured he lived in a neighborhood like mine, full of stray bikes lying abandoned on overgrown lawns and ranch-style houses with peeling wood siding. I definitely wasn't expecting all the landscaping and brick. His house—a two-story with a wraparound porch—sits on a huge, perfectly manicured lawn and is bordered by colorful flower beds full of azaleas and marigolds.

Alex pulls into the circular driveway. "Here we are."

I follow him up the front steps and onto the front porch to a big wooden front door. I wipe my pink Keds on the thick mat on the doorstep that says: *Bienvenidos*.

We walk into a huge, open room full of light from the

floor-to-ceiling windows. The furniture is comfortable, and it all matches in the way I've seen in magazines and home design television shows. Three people are sitting on the couch watching *My Super Sweet Sixteen* on a big-screen television. I recognize Alex's sister, Isabella, but I don't know the two older women. I can hear the total cost for the number-one *Super Sweet Sixteen* Blingest Bash on MTV adding up to the sound of a cash register. Thousands, no hundreds of thousands, of dollars. Izzy's mouth is open, her eyes glued to the television screen. She sits completely entranced by the sheer outrageousness and wonder of it all.

"You should be brought into the fiesta by a horse-drawn carriage," the smaller woman on the couch tells Isabella. "It has to be a gigantic entrance."

Isabella nods, but then the taller woman with the tight gray curls snaps her fingers like she has the best idea ever. "Maybe you should be carried in on the shoulders of some hot guys. You'd be inside this Cleopatra tent thingy on top of wooden poles," she says. "I saw that once on another episode."

The shorter woman says, "Maybe the guys should be really muscular so they can carry you."

"You think I'm *that* heavy?" Isabella asks in a way that makes it clear she knows it couldn't be farther from the truth.

Alex reaches for my hand. "This will go on forever if we don't interrupt. Come on. I'll introduce you."

I follow him across the room until we are standing in front of the TV and finally have the attention of the three people on the couch.

"Linden, this is my abuela Maria and her best friend, Mrs. Annie Florence."

I smile and give an awkward sort of half wave.

"And you already know my sister, Isabella," he says. Isabella is wearing purple shorts, a purple hoodie, and a purple T-shirt. Even the tiny rubber bands on her braces are purple. She looks back and forth between Alex and me, then leaps up off the couch and gives me an enthusiastic hug. It takes me by surprise, so I only hug back with one arm, but it doesn't seem to faze her.

"Aren't you a pretty girl," Mrs. Annie Florence, the taller woman with the gray curls, says, looking at me over the top of her blue polka-dotted half glasses. I feel my face catch fire at the inspection.

"Do you know my other grandson, Luis?" Abuela Maria asks me. "I think his girlfriend is your age. Torrey?"

I nod. "Yes, I know who she is."

"Such a sweet girl," she says, and Mrs. Annie Florence nods vigorously.

"We're planning my quinceañera," Isabella says, before flopping back down on the couch. She tells me the theme of her upcoming "sweet fifteen" celebration is Beauty and the Beast. According to her expert opinion, that is not nearly as obvious as Cinderella.

I smile. "Beauty and the Beast" is my favorite fairy tale. I love the idea of loving someone for who they are inside, even when no one else can see it.

"If you have a traditional quinceañera, people think it's boring," Isabella explains. "People expect a big production."

"Well, we can't have boring, that's for sure. Besides, you only turn fifteen once," Mrs. Annie Florence says. "You only get one chance to have a quinceañera."

"We have some candelabras at the funeral parlor that might work perfect for decorations," Abuela Maria says.

Alex explains to me, "My grandmother lives with my uncle and cousin Luis at the Rivera Funeral Home, but she spends a lot of time on our couch now that the party planning is at a fever pitch."

Sort of like prom?

Isabella makes a pouty face. "I don't want to use dead people's decorations."

"Why? They don't care," Abuela Maria says.

Alex tries to interrupt the conversation. "We're going to go study in my room."

Isabella ignores him, but I feel like I can't just walk away while she's talking. I shift from one foot to the other and she keeps chattering away.

"My court is going to do a waltz with me first, and then we're going to do a salsa, but sort of a hip-hop version," she says. "I have the most amazing choreographer."

"We need to verify everything with the florist. One red rose on each folded napkin," Abuela Maria says.

"Yes, and one rose under glass on each table for the centerpiece."

"Oh, yes! Perfect," says Mrs. Annie Florence, clapping her hands enthusiastically.

"It will be amazing," Isabella says.

I nod because it does sound incredible and also because they all seem so excited to share it with me.

"I could audition the attendants," Mrs. Annie Florence says.

"We both could. It wouldn't be any trouble," Alex's grandmother says, and Mrs. Annie Florence nods so hard all the gray curls on her head shake with enthusiasm.

Alex's grandmother punches her in the arm and grins; then they giggle like they are all fourteen.

Alex rolls his eyes. "Come on." He tugs at my hand.

Then, before we can walk away, Isabella stops us. "You know about the doll, right?" There is a beat of complete silence, and it takes a moment to realize everyone is looking at Alex. They are all three staring him down, so this must be important.

"What doll?" Alex asks.

"The brother of the birthday girl gives her a doll to signify she is leaving childhood behind," Abuela Maria says.

Mrs. Annie Florence nods her head again. I think it is

going to fall right off her pear-shaped body and roll under the couch.

"Lorin Lucero's quince doll is huge. It's in her bedroom," Isabella adds.

"Right. Doll," Alex says, and makes a check mark in the air. I follow him toward the stairs, but I can hear the conversation on the couch continuing all the way up the steps.

"Maybe you should have a cotton candy machine," Abuela Maria says. "I like cotton candy."

"Not sure how that will go with the theme," Isabella says. "But make a note of it."

CHAPTER TWELVE

Alex's room is cluttered but surprisingly clean, with a sunny window that looks out over a bricked-in patio and a pool. I stand there for a moment, taking it all in. Baseball is everywhere—posters of favorite players on his walls, mini trophies on his bookshelf, and signed baseballs inside plastic cases on his nightstand. There is a row of photos on top of his dresser, and I walk over to take a closer look. I recognize one of his sister and him when they were younger. They are standing on the beach with a boogie board propped up in the sand between them. They are grinning at the camera, squinting into the sun and covered with sand. Their smiles are the same, even now.

All of a sudden my heart is beating really fast, and all I'm thinking about is how cute Alex looks.

"Your sister is very pretty," I say, to take any potential attention off my flushed face.

Alex frowns. "Too pretty."

"What do you mean?" No one is ever *too* pretty. The beauty bar is set high, and it is always moving higher.

Better outfit. Curlier hair. Straighter hair. Short skirt. Long skirt. Bare skin. Tanned skin. High heels. Too high.

He picks up a baseball glove out of the window seat, pushes some athletic shoes out of the way, and motions for me to sit down. When I do, he sits cross-legged on the floor beside his bed, still holding the glove in one hand.

"She's always been oblivious to how she looks, but now she's starting to notice how others are looking at her. Especially boys," he says.

I know all about transformation. Not the dramatic, stepping-into-the-spotlight kind of transition Izzy will soon see. My change was much more gradual and not nearly as spectacular.

When I was Isabella's age, I was that kid in the background, with jeans that dragged around my feet and no thought of makeup. But then, when everyone came back to school the fall of their freshman year, suddenly my jeans weren't dragging around my pudgy legs anymore and, in fact, my legs weren't even pudgy. The front of my shirt stretched out with new curves, and whether I liked it or not, I was suddenly in the game.

"I see the way they look at her, and I don't want her to change." He is quiet for a minute. "At least not on the inside."

"I'm sorry," I say, but I don't really know why. I've never thought about it from a boy's perspective, but I know what pretty girls are like. This is how it works. We learn to get used to the looks, or at least we try. I glance at the picture

one more time. Isabella is going to have lots of guys looking, but there is no guarantee she will ever see herself in
the mirror the way they see her.

"When you came to the library the first time, you
described yourself as a good big brother."

"I think I am," he says. "It's just hard these days to
think about how to best support Isabella right now. There's
so much tradition to this quinceañera thing. It's all about
becoming a woman, but it's also tied to a lot of things that
seem so . . . " He pauses. "Superficial."

"Growing up as a girl can sometimes be complicated . . . "
I stumble for the right words, but Alex waits while I think.
"It's just . . . confusing." I shrug helplessly.

"Isn't growing up confusing for everybody?" Alex
asks.

"Sure. It's just that girls get so many messages from so
many different places—friends, television, internet." I tick
them off on my fingers. " 'Be grown up, but don't look
too grown up. Wear make-up, but don't look too made up.
Work out, but love your body the way it is. Be smart, but
don't act smart.' " I sigh. "That's only the tip of the iceberg."

Alex is silent for a moment, then he says, "I guess Izzy
is going through a lot."

I sit back in the window seat and Alex leans against
his bed, closing his eyes. I try not to think about how
the tops of his arms are so defined by muscle and how I
could just lean over and kiss him right now before he
even opens his eyes. But then he opens his eyes and I'm

caught. I swallow hard and quickly look down at my lap. My skirt is too short. I tug the hem of it down toward my knees for the fiftieth time. If I had worn tights I might have felt less exposed, but it is March in Texas and tights are out of the question.

When I glance back up, he's still looking at me. My stomach is doing something crazy, but I try to ignore it. "It sounds like Izzy's quinceañera is going to be a big deal," I say.

"The party planning had been going on for months, probably even years, but now it's down to the last few weeks. Every little detail is being analyzed and over-analyzed." He hits his fist into the palm of the glove. "Centerpieces. Dances. Dolls. I want nothing to do with any of it. But I can't ever say no to Izzy. No one can."

"I had no idea it was such a major event," I say, surprised at the emotion in his voice.

"Everything is about this party. Everything." He shakes his head. "Every dish my mom serves brings up the topic of what food we'll have and who is catering it. The laundry pile on the couch leads to talks of clothes and costumes. A song playing on the radio results in a lengthy conversation about music and the first dance— elaborately choreographed. Even the bouquet of flowers Sam brought home for my mom started this huge discussion about the flowers for the quince."

"Sam?" I ask.

"My stepdad," Alex says. "They met when he showed my mom some space for her newest restaurant. Sam was a horrible real estate agent. He said her eyes were the exact same color as the rusty pipes in the bathroom underneath the stained sink."

I laugh. "Smooth talker."

Alex finally smiles. "But for some reason known only to the two of them, it worked, and they were married six months later."

"How romantic," I say.

He shrugs. "Sam is the only dad I've ever known and he is pretty good at it, but sometimes he gets confused by all the traditions of our big Mexican family. Especially this quinceañera thing. He can never say anything right. If he says the caterer seems too expensive, then Isabella huffs off to her bedroom and won't speak to him for the rest of the evening. If he mentions a choice for the music, Abuela Maria goes crazy. It's a no-win situation, but it's like he can't help himself."

"And your real dad?" I ask.

"He died when I was little." Alex shakes his head.

"I'm sorry," I say.

"My mom and Sam argue a lot about Izzy's party. It's a lot of money and my mom wants it to be better than what she had, or better than any of her friends' daughters had. That is a lot of pressure, but she's one of the most competitive people on the planet."

I think about the pool outside in the backyard and the size of his house. Is money really an issue? Instead, I ask, "Is that where you get your competitiveness from?"

"I guess. I've always loved baseball, but no one else saw me as being good enough to really play. I was always too little or too slow." He picks up the ball lying on the floor beside him and wraps his fingers around it. "But this year is different. It's like everything clicked."

I saw how everyone in the stands at the baseball field reacted at the game. Alex was amazing.

"Your mother must be proud," I say.

"I don't know." He shrugs. "She hasn't been to one of my games yet. She's either doing something for Izzy's quinceañera or at the restaurant trying to make the money to pay for it."

"Well, it sounds like that doll is going to be even better than Lorin Lucero's." I try to tease him to lighten the mood.

He laughs. "According to my sister, Lorin Lucero's quinceañera is the standard by which all other birthday parties are measured. *Everybody* knows that."

I smile. "Obviously."

There's a knock at the door.

"Come in," Alex calls.

A dark-haired woman with Alex's smile stands at the door. "I heard you had a friend over."

"Mom, this is Linden."

The woman in the doorway is wearing a sleeveless blue

eyelet dress and white open-toed heels. Her makeup is flawless and her bright red lipstick looks freshly applied. I wish I'd worn something nicer besides this short skirt and T-shirt. I stand up from my seat in the window. I'm not sure if I should shake her hand or not, so I give her this little half wave. "Nice to meet you, Mrs. Rivera."

So awkward.

She doesn't seem fazed. "You too, Linden. I wanted to ask you to join us for dinner."

My mom is at the firehouse, so everyone will probably be on their own for dinner at my house. "Sure," I say, though my stomach does a little wobble at the idea.

"Well, finish up your homework and come down in about thirty minutes," she says. She leaves the door open when she walks away.

Alex shrugs at the open door, grinning at me, and instantly I think about kissing him in my front yard. I can feel a giggle bubbling up inside of me, but I don't want to look like some kind of loon, so I hide it by walking across the room and picking up my book bag.

We settle onto the floor and study for the next half hour until my phone buzzes.

NIKKI: ASK HIM ABOUT PROM!

I exit out of the message. Now doesn't seem the time.

"Who's that?" Alex asks.

"Just Nikki," I say. "I'll call her later."

Later, I sit at the dining room table thinking this is the way family dinners should be—noisy and crowded. Abuela Maria decides to stay over for dinner, which evidently isn't unusual, but Mrs. Annie Florence says she has to go home to perfect her dewberry cobbler recipe for the upcoming Walker County Fair.

Alex introduces me to Sam, his stepdad, who sits next to Isabella, and the conversation continues as though I am not even there, but not in a bad way. I take a long sip of iced tea and let the words blur around me, but then I feel Alex reach for my hand under the table. He squeezes it, gently, looking straight ahead.

"Mom, Alex is smiling at the potatoes. Weird," Izzy says.

"Alex, why are you smiling at the potatoes?" his mom asks, putting a piece of meat loaf on my plate, even though I didn't ask for it.

"Sorry. I didn't know I wasn't allowed to smile. I won't do it again."

"There, Isabella," Mrs. Rivera says. "Your brother won't be smiling at vegetables anymore."

"Maybe it's because he has a girlfriend," Isabella says slyly. "Love makes you stupid."

My cheeks burst into flame.

"Ouch." Isabella turns to Sam. "Alex kicked me."

"Don't tease your brother, Izzy," Sam says, stabbing at his meat. "It's his business."

For the moment, the spotlight is off us, and I slowly relax into my chair. I'm glad Isabella drops it and shifts the topic to her upcoming quinceañera. Alex is right. It's the focus of everything. The conversation buzzes on. Alex's grandmother and mother talk in Spanish about the order of the ceremony, with Izzy throwing in comments in English every so often.

"What do you think, Sam?" Isabella asks. Sam and Alex both freeze with forks halfway to mouths. I take a bite of meat loaf and chew slowly, feeling the shift in mood.

"About what?" Sam still doesn't look up from his plate.

"The crown!" Izzy says. "Should I have one or not?"

"I think you call it a tiara," Abuela Maria says.

"How much does it cost?" Sam asks, then seems to realize he said the wrong thing once again, so he quickly adds, "Just wondering."

"Don't worry, *mija*," Alex's mom says, reaching out to stroke Izzy's hair. "Money is not a problem."

Sam's neck gets red and blotchy.

"Never mind," he says.

Alex's mom gives him a look that makes me feel sorry for him, and the redness spreads up his neck to his ears.

"My quinceañera was so much simpler. Just the mass and a cake," Abuela Maria says. "Now you have to have costume changes and limos." She laughs. "My mom made my dress. The party was in the church hall, and my family prepared the food—tamales, beans, and rice. We had mariachis and I danced with my cousins."

"I'm sure it was perfect, but things are different now," Alex's mom says. "I've been planning this party since the moment Izzy was born, so money is no object. We will find you the most beautiful tiara in the history of quinces. Won't we, Sam?"

Sam nods slowly and stuffs another piece of meat loaf in his mouth. He hasn't said much since we sat down, and now the pale white skin on the back of his neck turns red again.

"What song should we play for the brother-sister dance?" Isabella asks.

"We have to dance together?" Alex asks.

"We talked about this, Alex. You've been practicing the dance, right?" Her voice gets higher and higher until probably only the dogs in the neighborhood can hear it. "Mom, Alex has been practicing, right?"

"Of course he has," his mom says. "Haven't you, Alex?"

Alex grins at Isabella across the table and she sticks her tongue out at him.

"It's not funny," she said. "The very first dance will be the brother-sister dance, and it has to be perfect."

Alex's smile vanishes. "I thought the first dance was supposed to be the father-daughter dance," he says. He looks over at Sam, who is very intently staring at his meat loaf.

"I'm not that good of a dancer," he mumbles. He knew about this.

Sam's neck turns even redder, and I can't help but feel sorry for him.

"You're going to do the first dance, and Sam will change my shoes," Isabella says. Sam darts a look at Alex, then focuses back on rearranging the slice of meat loaf on his plate.

I have no idea what she is talking about. Evidently, Alex's grandmother realizes it about the same time, so she explains, "After the first dance, the birthday girl's father takes off her flats and replaces them with high heels more befitting a young lady."

"I can do that," Sam says quickly. Alex gives him a squinty-eyed look, but Sam ignores him.

Isabella's phone makes a dinging noise.

"I've told you no phones at the dinner table," her mom says.

"I'll turn it off," Izzy says, pulling it out of her pocket. She looks down at the screen. "It's this new app I downloaded called Worthy."

I'm surprised Izzy knows about Worthy, but I shouldn't be. It's a sure sign something has spread to the whole school when even freshmen are joining in.

"It's like a favorite-couple contest. Everybody decides whether they're worthy of each other or not," Izzy says.

Alex rolls his eyes.

Her mom looks down at Izzy's phone. "Just some new craziness," she says. "Now put it away and eat your dinner."

She's right. It is crazy. I *know* it. So why am I wondering what the notification was from Worthy?

WORTHY

Hey, Hornets. Tick. Tock. It's that time again. Another girl is coming up for your review. Let me know what you think . . . I can't wait, can you?

CHAPTER THIRTEEN

The next morning, I stare down at my phone, my cereal growing mushy in the bowl. I'm seriously sleep deprived. I stayed up way too late last night, pinning promposals on Pinterest and checking Worthy for updates. There have been no more alerts, but every possible form of social media is exploding with the possible names of the next target. This morning I feel the guilt scuttle under my skin again, slinking deeper. Kat was right. Maybe I didn't post mean comments about Raylene, but I became part of the Worthy mania by voting.

My open journal mocks me with empty pages. I pick up my pen and write the first words that come to mind.

Nasty. Cruel. Malicious. Shameful.

"Everything okay, Linden?" Mom is hovering over the toaster. No cooking-show fails this morning. Our kitchen is much smaller than Alex's, with a table in a nook by the windows where we eat all our meals and magnets covering the fridge from vacation destinations. There is no view of a swimming pool in the backyard. Just a patio table and a couple of chairs that have definitely seen way too many summers. "You're looking pretty grim this morning."

"I'm fine. Just sleepy."

Two Pop-Tarts spring up from the toaster, and Mom gingerly fishes one out. "Want one?"

I shake my head. "Where's Dad?"

"He took your brother to school early on his way to work. Theodore had some kind of club meeting."

"When does your shift start?" I ask.

"Today. I won't be home for a couple of nights. Move," she says to Murphy, who repositions himself from under her feet to a prime spot under the table. She sits down beside me, takes a bite, and then puffs out air around her now open mouth. "Hot," she says.

I nod, chewing on a spoonful of Cheerios.

She reaches out and smooths my hair back behind one ear. "You sure everything is okay?"

I look up from the phone. Mom's eyes are the same as mine—light golden brown that looks almost green in the right light—but sometimes I think that's all we share. "Yeah, I'm sure."

My phone buzzes and I look back down at the screen.

NIKKI: DID ALEX ASK YOU TO PROM?

I click my phone off and swallow hard, then turn it over on the table.

That afternoon we have a junior class assembly. Alex slides into the seat beside me, giving me a quick kiss. This time our lips touch confidently, like we greet each other like this all the time. I don't jerk away, but I still feel a little self-conscious. It's the first real sign to the world that we're dating, and there's nothing more public than a school assembly. I sneak a peek at him, checking to see if he looks uncomfortable, but he doesn't.

At first, the assembly is pretty ordinary. The candidates for student council president give their election speeches. Max is definitely the front-runner. His speech is full of promises about healthier options in the cafeteria and student input on the school calendar. The only other candidate is Emma Johnson. She plays trombone and has a strong band following, but she is still a long shot.

Then Heather makes an announcement about prom and urges everyone to get their tickets before they sell out. Alex is sitting beside me, and I give him a sideways look to see if he reacts at all to the prom announcement, but he just stares straight ahead. Nikki is sitting on the other side of me and she nudges me with her elbow. I ignore her.

At the end, Mrs. Hernandez, the principal, comes up, and I can tell something is different by the way she taps at the microphone at least five times to make sure everyone is listening. The loud feedback screech makes everyone clap hands over ears and groan.

When it finally dies down, Mrs. Hernandez clears her

throat and says, "It has come to our attention that there is a malicious online app being circulated throughout the student body."

Raylene and Ross are sitting three rows in front of me, and I see people twisting around in their seats to look at them. Ross's arm is around Raylene's shoulders and his expression is grim. Raylene has a weird smile plastered on her face that looks more like she's screaming than actually smiling. Her hair is flat and scraped back into a ponytail. She isn't wearing her signature bling or anything at all that would command attention. I look away, feeling sad for the loss of everything Raylene.

Alex reaches for my hand and links our fingers together. He gives my hand a squeeze and I look down. I've seen Alex throw a baseball at lightning speeds, and I know the strength in that hand. But right now, sitting in the middle of this auditorium, he is cradling mine in his with the lightest of touches. I glance up at his profile and suddenly I'm a big puddle of mush. This is who I want to be holding in my arms, slow dancing with under the sparkling lights. And in that moment, I decide: I *will* ask Alex to the prom. It's time for me to stop making up fairy tales when I have a chance to actually live one.

The wonder of my decision buzzes around in my brain so loudly that I can hardly concentrate on the stage, but Mrs. Hernandez continues, "We want to encourage anyone who feels bullied online or in person to report it to your teachers or to me."

A few kids look at the person next to them in confusion and are quickly filled in with whispered information. A wave of murmured conversation ripples around the auditorium, and Mrs. Hernandez taps the microphone again.

"We will also be sending a letter to all parents to encourage their involvement in order to stop the spread of this vicious activity," Mrs. Hernandez says. "If you have information about who is behind this app, I implore you to speak up and stand up for your fellow students."

The assembly ends and everyone files out. Everywhere I look, students are pulling phones out of purses, backpacks, and pockets on their way out the door. I can't help but think this big shot of extra publicity will result in even more downloads and shares than ever. I resolve that for the rest of the day, I will not check Worthy.

When I'm leaving the library later that afternoon, my phone buzzes with a text from Nikki.

NIKKI: COME OVER AFTER WORK! VERY IMPORTANT!!!

Three exclamation points. Something must definitely be up.

I drive straight to Nikki's house. I walk into her bedroom to find Maricel is sitting in the middle of the floor. Her eyes are red and she's crying.

"What's up?" I ask, feeling like I walked in on a movie already in progress. I look at Nikki, sitting on the floor beside her, and she shrugs. I perch myself on the side of the bed, pull out a candy bar from my bag, and wait until Maricel's tears subside enough for her to talk.

Finally, between her sobs, Maricel says, "Donnie Robinson said I was fat and ugly."

"Are you fat?" Nikki asks her.

Maricel looks at her, surprised enough by the question to stop crying. "No."

"Are you ugly?"

"No."

"So what does it matter what Donnie Robinson says?"

It seems so simple when Nikki puts it that way, but it isn't. Learning to love yourself can be a very difficult task. For me, it's a daily contest to find that kind of confidence. I unwrap the candy bar and break off a piece.

Maricel pauses, then asks in a much softer voice, "But what if . . . " She looks at Nikki, then drops her eyes.

"You *were* fat?" Nikki asks. "Like me?"

Maricel nods.

Nikki laughs, but I can hear a touch of bitterness in it. "Then you need to get a thicker skin."

Maricel's eyes widen. "You don't care what people think about you?"

"Of course I care. But I can't change what goes on in other people's heads," Nikki says. She leans over to brush the hair out of Maricel's face.

"And if you love what's in here . . . " She taps her sister's chest. "Really, really love it . . . " Nikki stands up and holds out her hand. "Then no one has the power to make you feel ugly. No matter what."

Not even Jake Edwards? I want to ask.

Maricel takes the outstretched hand and Nikki pulls her up off the floor. It's the perfect pep talk for every teen girl. I could give Maricel some advice, too, but the messages that slither around in my head aren't nearly that clear.

Stand up straight, but not too tall.

Be strong, but not muscular.

Wear the stylish clothes and great outfits, but don't put too much emphasis on shallow things like that.

Be everything for everyone.

But who am I to contradict someone who has figured it all out?

"By the way, I've decided I don't like Miguel Canino after all," she tells me.

"Why not? I thought he was adorbs." I use her terminology.

Sighing, she says, "We rode our bikes home from school yesterday and he never asked me a single question. Not one."

"And that's important because?"

Her eyes go narrow. "If a guy doesn't ask anything, then they don't really want to get to know you," she says.

"You might be right." I am surprised at her intuition. "So who *do* you like?"

"I don't have to like anyone," she says firmly. "Life isn't all about boys, Linden."

I feel a spark of hope. Maybe Maricel is going to be all right after all. For a minute, I wish I were ten again. I pull her in for a bear hug, rubbing the top of her head until her hair sticks out in a tangled mess. She gives a shrieky laugh and squirms away. I smile at her and then give her a little shove.

Nikki waves her toward the door. "Linden and I have some private stuff to talk about. Okay?"

"I gotta bounce," Maricel tells me like it is totally her idea to leave. Then she walks out of the room, closing the door behind her.

Nikki sighs and looks over at me. "You're eating chocolate, so everything with Alex must be going well."

"It's going great," I say. But I don't divulge all the details. I want to keep some of the amazingness all to myself, to think about when I turn the lights off at night.

Nikki picks up a glass from her nightstand and takes a swig of green liquid, instantly making a face.

"Why are you drinking that stuff?"

"I want to lose ten pounds by prom. Speaking of prom, did Alex ask you?"

"No one at his house even remembers there's a prom coming up. It's just not on the radar right now with all his sister's quinceañera stuff."

Nikki shakes her head. "That's too bad."

"It's going to be fine, though," I say, leaning back against the headboard of her bed. "Because I have a plan."

"Why does that not surprise me?"

"I'm going to ask him"—I pause for dramatic effect—"with the biggest promposal yet."

Her mouth falls open. "Are you serious?"

I nod. "You think I'm crazy?"

"Absolutely, but this is going to be fantastic. Have you figured out how you're going to do it?"

"I've been researching it on Pinterest," I say, feeling my excitement grow. "And I think I'm going to get some people to hold up a big banner at the baseball field. It's a huge game and everyone will be there. I'll get someone to film it, of course."

Nikki smiles at me and holds out a fist. "Good for you, Linden. I didn't think you had it in you."

I totally have it in me. Maybe I always have. I bump my own fist against hers and grin back. After years of being in everyone's shadow, I'm stepping into the spotlight. I deserve this.

Nikki sits down beside me on the side of the bed. "I have some big news, too. Guess who just went up on Worthy?"

I plump up the pillow more behind me on the bed and break off another square of chocolate. "Who?"

She puts her hands on my shoulders and leans into my face, her eyes wide. "Me and Jake!"

I choke on chocolate and cough. "You?" I stammer. "And Jake?"

No no no no no. This can't be happening. If people were cruel to Raylene, what will they do to Nikki?

Nikki seems oblivious to my panic. "I know, right? It's probably because Jake is a senior, but it's still cool, right?"

"I guess so . . . " I can't believe Nikki thinks this is a good idea.

"You don't sound so sure," she says. She picks up her phone off her nightstand and clicks to the already open app. "Look. They picked a good picture of us."

I stare down at Nikki's smiling face under the now all-too-familiar question, "Is she worthy?"

"And Jake looks amazing, don't you think? Of course, he never takes a bad picture . . . "

I glance up from the phone. "You're different around Jake." I say it before I can stop myself.

"I've never dated anyone like him before." She's still looking down at the phone with that weird half smile on her face.

"You mean popular?" I ask.

"Yeah, I guess so," Nikki says. "I never thought someone like him would like someone like me. The fat girl gets the popular guy. It just doesn't happen that way."

"That's not a reason to go out with him," I say. *Where did this come from?* I'm thinking. Nikki has always been the one who believed in herself no matter what, but now I'm seeing huge cracks in her confidence that I've never seen before.

"I know," she says. "But I like how I feel when I'm with him. Like I'm special."

Now I'm angry. Didn't she just tell Maricel the opposite? "You don't need him for that, Nikki." I spit out the words.

She frowns. "I didn't think so, but now I'm not so sure."

Just when I think Nikki has everything figured out, she surprises me. We have shared everything from first crushes to the death of beloved grandparents. But I can't share how it feels to be inside Nikki's skin. I let out a big sigh.

"Don't get caught up in this Worthy thing," I plead with her.

It's like she doesn't even hear me. "I know I'm going to be a long shot. After all, Jake is gorgeous."

So are you.

"And he's a senior," she continues. "Every girl in school would love to go out with him."

Not everyone.

"And he likes me," she adds. She takes another swig of the green concoction and then says, "I'm just not sure about his friends. I don't think they really accept me." She gives a nervous laugh. "I guess we'll know soon enough. Worthy will be the judge of that."

"What other people think shouldn't matter," I say, unable to keep the frustration out of my voice. *Haven't you told me that a million times?*

She looks sideways at me. "Admit it. You don't think we should be together either. No one does."

Guilt stabs me in the stomach. She's right. I don't think they should be together. Nikki is way too good for Jake.

Nikki stands up from the bed and walks over to the desk. "If *we* think we're a match, it doesn't matter what other people say." It's like she's trying to talk herself into believing it.

I open my mouth, but don't speak.

Her brief lapse in confidence is gone and her voice rises as she stalks around the room punching the air with one finger for emphasis.

"This Worthy thing isn't going to beat me. You'll see." She stops in the middle of the room and glares at me. "I decided a long time ago that if people were going to stare at me, I'd give them something to look at, and now everyone's going to be looking." She stops suddenly and sinks onto her bed, holding her phone limp in her hand. "Whether I like it or not," she whispers.

WORTHY

Whoa! Looks like we have a BIG
competition brewing with this one,
peeps (get it???). Don't be left out.
This vote is going to be HUGE!
Bring it on.

CHAPTER FOURTEEN

"Your mom called from the fire station," my dad says when I walk into the kitchen that night. "The cook-off thing went great. Her team won."

He hovers over the stove, stirring a frying pan with a big wooden spoon. My brother sits at the kitchen table, long legs stretched out into the chair across from him. He wears a black T-shirt with a pi symbol on the front, jeans, and a pair of Vans Super Mario Brothers slip-ons. He is talking to my dad about monarch butterflies, which is not unusual for Rat.

My brother grins at me and runs one hand through his blond, spiky hair. "Did you know the ancient Aztecs of central Mexico believed the monarch butterflies were the souls of their fallen warriors?"

"Nope," I say, pouring iced tea into a glass. It is also not unusual that I have no idea what he is talking about.

Tonight, I *really* don't have room in my head for Rat's randomness. All the way home from Nikki's, I tried to make some sense of our conversation, but I was still struggling. I also have been keeping to my resolution to not check Worthy today. Especially now. I don't want to see what people are saying about Nikki in the comments. My stomach tightens.

Dad turns off the stove and looks our way. "Will you set the table, Theodore?" he asks, and my brother gets up to pull down dishes and collect silverware.

"Are you and Ever going to prom?" I ask Rat, sitting down in front of one of the place settings.

"Absolutely," Rat says. "That's what made me think of butterflies."

I look at him blankly.

"Transformation?" he asks as though it is totally obvious.

I still don't have a clue. Taking a long drink of iced tea, I just wait. He will explain himself eventually.

"I have to get my tux ordered and will soon"—he laughs, waving his long arms around—"transform into a gorgeous butterfly."

"Well, you're certainly in a good mood this evening, Theodore." My dad places the skillet on a hot pad in the middle of the table, then looks over at me. "And you're certainly not, Linden."

I look up, my glass halfway to my mouth. Was it that obvious? "I just have a lot on my mind."

"Like what?" Rat asks.

Alex. Prom. Nikki. Worthy.

It is all jumbled up and way too complicated to explain, so I just say, "My history test is tomorrow."

We eat sloppy joes for dinner. It is one of my dad's go-to dishes, and it tastes better than any of the elaborate recipes my mother creates. Murphy is in his familiar spot by my right leg. I slip him a piece of bread under the table and I hear the grateful swish of his tail against the floor.

"How about we watch a movie tonight? Anything you want," my dad says.

"I can't," I say. "I've got a ton of homework. History test, remember?"

He turns to my brother. "Theo?"

"Sorry. Chemistry club meeting, and then I have to pick up Ever from her musical rehearsal."

Dad's shoulders slump. "And your mom's at the firehouse until Monday night."

He looks so alone, it makes me worry. Everyone is going their own way. We aren't even a family anymore. Rat stands up and picks up his book bag off the chair next to him. He grabs a chocolate chip cookie off the kitchen countertop and takes a bite on his way out the door. "I'll be home pretty late," he calls back over his shoulder. Then it is just me and Dad.

"Are you okay with Mom's new job?" I ask. He looks startled at my question.

"Why?"

"She's just gone a lot and we don't do anything as a family anymore. Not even eat dinner." I think about the crowded table at Alex's house, and it makes me feel like something's missing.

Dad gives a little laugh and picks up the plates off the table. "Your mom never cooked dinner anyway."

"But we ate together," I say. "Every night."

"Yeah, I miss that, too." He sighs. "But your mom is doing what she wants to do, and that makes a couple of nights at home alone totally worth it, right?"

"I guess so," I say. "But don't you get tired of being the one always left behind?"

Is this what's happening with Nikki? I think as I stand up with my plate. *But is she leaving me behind, or am I leaving her?*

Either way, it doesn't feel right.

"Being a firefighter is her big dream, and we're going to do everything we can as a family to support her," Dad says, heading toward the kitchen. "Even if it takes some sacrifices."

I'm proud of my firefighter mom, but I want her to still be my mom, too. And tonight I really wish I could talk to her. Instead, I rinse off the plates in the sink and load the dishwasher. Just as I put in the last glass, my phone buzzes.

I pull it out of my pocket. It's an unfamiliar number, but I quickly realize it's from Taylor. I enter her name into my phone, which feels kind of exciting.

TAYLOR: THE SHOE HASHTAG IS FAB! U R BRILLIANT

ME: THANKS

TAYLOR: CAN'T WAIT TO SEE WHAT'S NEXT

Taylor is texting me? I didn't even know she knew my number. Today has been bizarre. I feel edgy. Jittery. I need to clear my head.

"I'm going to take the dog for a quick walk before it gets dark," I tell Dad, and he waves at me over the back of the couch. When I snap the leash onto Murphy's collar, he does a little celebration circle, looking up at me to be sure we are ready to go.

Outside, I put on my sneakers and sit down on the bench beside the garage to tie them. It's hot and muggy. Murphy sits on the driveway, sniffing the air and waiting. He is oblivious to my mood. I can't blame him for not noticing. An evening walk is one of his favorite things in the world. Except for maybe car rides and treats. Okay, definitely treats are number one, and then the whole riding in the car with the window down is definitely number two. Tennis balls would reluctantly be assigned number three. If only my life were so simple.

I start walking toward the trail that comes after the dead end. When I hit the trail I speed up, starting to sweat, but I can't shake the thoughts running through my head. I turn the corner at the bend in the trail and head downhill. I pull the air deep into my lungs and walk even faster. The heat is building, pressing in against my body, pushing down my throat. All my thoughts keep pace, racing along with me.

I first realized Nikki's size made her feel different one

day when we were thirteen and shopping at the mall. We were picking out jeans with some friends. She picked out the largest size, but they still didn't fit. I remember the way she looked when she tried to tug them up around hips that were already way curvier than any of ours. No matter how hard she squeezed and pulled at the zipper, the jeans wouldn't go up. She begged me not to tell the other girls.

I knew she felt strange about going around the racks of clothes to the farthest sizes, so I went with her—pulling out some for her to try on. She hated every single pair. At the end of the day, the other girls and I had shopping bags filled with tank tops, miniskirts, jeans, and dresses. In Nikki's bag, she had some sandals and a flowered scarf. Left behind on the shelves were skirts that were too tight, blouses that didn't meet at the buttons, and boots that didn't zip over her calves. All her choices were so slim.

Nikki could have given up and slunk off to the sidelines, but she was always a fighter and never set foot on a sideline in her life. So the next time we went shopping, she marched right over to the biggest sizes. If she couldn't find what she wanted, she vowed to make it herself. Instead of being ashamed of her body, she celebrated her curves in every way imaginable. That's one of the things I loved most about her. Still do. But maybe I didn't realize how hard this fight has been.

Finally, I stop, panting and leaning hard into the pecan tree at the edge of the trail. For a long moment, I just breathe, bending over at the waist with one hand on the tree for balance. I wipe the sweat out of my eyes with my T-shirt and look down at Murphy, panting happily at my side.

"Good boy." Murphy's tail waves enthusiastically. His furry doggy eyebrows raise in question and he grins his happy dog smile. "You don't have to talk to be happy. You just have to be you."

I walk over and sit on top of a picnic table, staring at the creek gurgling over a patch of stark white boulders. Murphy climbs up and sits beside me. Nikki has been my constant through everything. But who am I without her? The thought is terrifying. There's a reason I love shoes so much. I've spent way too much time looking down at the ground.

"Taylor Reed likes me," I tell Murphy. "It's a good thing to have more friends, right?"

Murphy leans his head against my shoulder. His tail thumps.

I eventually throw three round, smooth rocks into the water, one after the other, with long, quiet pauses in between. Murphy holds himself back from splashing out into the water, but I can tell it is almost impossible. His bottom wiggles anxiously, but he keeps it planted firmly on the tabletop right beside my leg. But, just in case, his golden eyes carefully track the path of each rock through the late evening sun from the moment it leaves my hand until it disappears beneath the shimmering surface.

My computer sits open on my desk, giving me the evil eye. Ever since I've taken on this social media job for prom, I haven't written a word on my story and the deadline is only two weeks away. I glance at my overflowing book-shelves, stacked high with so many well-loved stories, and sigh. My dream of writing something worthy of going on that bookcase is flickering out. Like a helium birthday balloon escaping the bunch into a bright blue sky. The string just out of reach. Grasping. Reaching. Just missed.

I get into my pajamas and brush my hair back from my face into a big, messy ponytail. Taking out my contacts, I put them in the case and find my glasses. The computer still waits. Pinned to the wall above it is my writing calendar. I read somewhere it was a good motivational tool to put a sticker on a calendar for every day you wrote something. So far, there are only three tiny flower stickers on the whole month. I sigh.

Reluctantly, I flop down at my desk, but my eyes drift to the open window. In two weeks the moon will be full. Just in time for prom. A perfect backdrop for a magical evening. The lamppost outside casts a long shadow across the lawn, reminding me of Alex and kissing. Suddenly, there is no room in my brain for anything else. I smile.

Then I squeeze my eyes tightly closed, giving myself a two-second mental pep talk. When I open them, I stare down at the blank page. Ready to go.

I turn on my playlist and the music is incredibly tempting, sucking me in with the soft slap of the drum and the seductive bass sliding up and down the scale. Norah Jones. Smooth. Whispering of a life I think I'll never know, with jazz and outdoor cafés and brunches with Fendi sunglasses and strappy Kate Spade sandals, drinking out of glasses that have stems.

I look down at my hands. Unfortunately, the fingernail polish on my thumbnail is chipped. Completely distracting. I stand up. It takes me a while to track down the right color of polish, the fingernail polish remover, a cotton ball. I repaint the nail to perfection. All the while I think through exactly how my big plan to ask Alex to prom is going to play out. I'll make the banner this week and ask Taylor to help hold it up at the game. I will have two balloons at the edge of the banner. One red balloon that says "No." And one green balloon that says "Yes." Alex will pick the "Yes" one, of course, and I'll let the "No" one go to float up into the air while the crowd cheers. Then we'll kiss. And it will be perfect.

Don't think about kissing Alex.

My story is still waiting, but now I'm totally thinking about kissing Alex again. My phone buzzes with a text and jerks me out of my daydream.

NIKKI: DON'T FORGET TO VOTE. I'M BEHIND. ☹
ME: K

There is a humming in my ears. Thinking about Worthy makes me feel guilty for supporting that stupid app. But then all I can think of is how Jake is making Nikki different. If everyone says she should be with him, then it is going to make things even worse. She isn't worthy of him because he is an arrogant, conceited jerk. She doesn't deserve a guy like that. Saying yes to Worthy is limiting her to guys like Jake who want to change everything about her.

She's worth so much more.

I shiver suddenly—an impulsive jerk that takes me by surprise. The buzz in my head is now at a fever pitch. I pull out my phone, click to Nikki and Jake's picture on Worthy, and before I can talk myself out of it, I choose NO.

Nikki Aquino & Jake Edwards

IS SHE WORTHY?

Here's what you are saying:

* I can't believe he's dating her! No way.

* Honey! Eat less. Exercise more.

* I guess more is better. Right, Jake??

* Why shouldn't she date him? She's big and beautiful. Good for him.

CHAPTER FIFTEEN

I knew Nikki wouldn't hide from the attention, but I never expected this. She is waiting for me at the front door when I get to school. She takes off her cardigan and I stare. Her neon-orange tee is printed with a question in huge black block letters: AM I GOOD ENOUGH?

I'm stunned. "How did you do that?"

"I stayed up late last night making it. What do you think?"

I think I am a horrible friend. My stomach clenches. "Wow," I say.

I tried to change my vote this morning, but the app wouldn't accept it.

It's anonymous. She'll never know.

But I know, and it is eating away at me. The crowd of students are pushing in through the glass doors and Nikki stands there in the midst of them passing out little glittery heart stickers. "I'm not going down without a fight," she tells me, and hands me a sheet of stickers to pass out.

Nikki steps in front of a girl carrying an instrument case. "Do you think I'm good enough?"

The girl looks at her in shock, then stammers, "Ummm. Sure."

"Then choose the heart on Worthy," Nikki says, and hands the girl a sticker.

The door opens, and Jake walks in with a couple of other senior boys. My heart drops. I can't bear to see their reaction to Nikki's campaign.

"Hey, babe." He walks up to Nikki and leans down for a quick kiss. He turns to the other boys and says, "This is what I was talking about. Everyone wears these hearts, right?"

They nod, and Nikki hands them stickers, beaming. I'm in shock. She told Jake about this last night and she didn't tell me? But worse, he is supporting her when I did not. Jake flashes his way too gorgeous smile at me. The group of senior boys heads off down the hall with extra stickers in hand, but Jake stays behind to help Nikki.

"You are so brave," one girl tells Nikki.

I back away and bump right into Blair Cunningham, the biggest stylista in the whole junior class and one of the most fashionable of the Lovelies. She makes a huge huffy puffy noise, like I couldn't possibly be more clumsy.

"Sorry," I say, reaching out to steady Blair.

She glares at me and my hands drop to my sides. "Watch where you're going."

Nikki steps in between us, looking Blair up and down. "It was an accident."

Blair rolls her eyes. "Whatever."

She starts to walk away, but Nikki stops her. "You know, that dress would look better on you if you took the sleeves off."

Everyone within earshot sucks in their breath and waits for Blair to explode. No one critiques Blair. Especially not on her high-end fashion sense.

But when Nikki says "Never mind" and starts to turn away, Blair comes after her. Mia, a tiny little shadow, follows at a safe distance.

"Are you messing with me?" Blair demands.

"No, I'm . . . "

The crowd surrounds them, whispering and waiting.

"I know you." Blair snaps her fingers in the air. "You're the new girl on Worthy. I like your style."

I can hear the murmurs around the circle of kids watching. "Blair Cunningham likes her style?"

"Could you do it?" Blair asks, stepping up into Nikki's face.

"What?" Nikki is confused, but not intimidated.

"Make the dress work?"

"Sure," Nikki says.

"You are amazing," Blair says. "And this whole thing . . . " She points to Nikki's shirt. "Is genius."

"Do you want a sticker?"

"Absolutely." Blair places it right on her shoulder for everyone to see.

"I'll see you after third period," Nikki calls back to me over her shoulder. Then, wonder of wonders, they walk off together, leaving me and Mia behind to watch with our mouths hanging open.

"I'm thinking if you cut the neckline more into a scoop, it would show off your shoulder blades to perfection . . . "

"Are you sure?" I hear Blair ask.

As soon as Nikki leaves with Blair, the other girls put their heads together and start whispering. I watch them, but I don't say anything. It amazes me to see how suddenly Nikki has apparently become the newest thing. This is the same crowd that I've watched make fun of the outcasts, like Tomas Myers, who continually rocks to his own internal playlist, and Deb Shefield, who is probably smarter than the whole junior class put together, but has some annoying habits, like sucking her teeth endlessly.

I hope you know what you're doing, Nikki.

After third period, I wait for Nikki and entertain myself with shoes. A pair of snakeskin cowboy boots stand next to a pair of beat-up yellow loafers. A pair of big Nike athletic shoes with the laces untied stand in front of lockers. A pair of red heels walks past and the sneakers follow quickly. A locker door slams and I look up. Instantly, I get goose bumps. There are heart stickers everywhere—on hoodies, dresses, T-shirts, and even foreheads.

"Can you believe it?" Nikki stands beside me. "We are

freaking awesome." She gives me that brilliant smile that would make anyone feel instantly better.

Except for a horrible friend like me.

"Me and Jake are going to take our lunch outside and eat on the grass. Everyone will see us together."

"And comment?" I ask.

She lets out a laugh, then shrugs. "You got to do what you got to do."

I have to tell her what I did. "Nikki . . . " I start to say.

Jake materializes out of thin air. "Want to join us?"

I shake my head. "Not today."

I watch them walk away together in the wake of swiveling heads and whispered, behind-the-hands comments.

Between third and fourth periods, Mrs. Boggs stops me in the hall. "Linden, can I talk to you a minute?"

It must be about my vocabulary test. I knew I should have studied more, but I totally ran out of time. Mrs. Boggs sits down at her desk and pats the empty chair beside her. She looks way too serious for one freaking quiz grade. I slump into the seat and fold my hands in my lap, waiting.

"I wanted to talk to you about this app everyone's using."

My head snaps up. In a split second, I decide to play dumb. "What app?"

Mrs. Boggs sighs. She isn't buying it. "You were at the assembly last week and you know what I'm talking about, Linden."

I look down at my carefully folded hands. My thumbs tap against each other restlessly.

"Do you know who created it?" she asks.

I look up and lock eyes with her. "No," I say. "No one knows."

"I'm sorry. This kind of judgment must feel very invasive for your friend, Nikki," Mrs. Boggs says, shaking her head. "I just want you to know that I'm here if you, or if anyone you know, wants to talk about it."

"Thanks, Mrs. B. I'm sure the attention will just move on to someone else." It is a good answer and I hope it is true. I stand and pick my backpack up off the floor.

"If you know who's doing this, Linden, please let me know," Mrs. Boggs says before I can walk away. "Speaking up about something like this isn't tattling. It's taking a stand to stop it."

I shoulder my book bag and turn for the door. "I have no idea how to stop it, Mrs. B. If I did, I would."

In the cafeteria, Max sets a small metal lockbox down on the table covered in green and gold tissue-paper streamers. Behind him are two handmade posters taped up on the wall featuring prom shoe pictures and details about the contest.

"Great idea, Linden," he says as I approach. "You should be my campaign manager. Or better yet, your friend out there should be. She's got everyone talking." He bobs his head toward the courtyard. When I look over his shoulder, I see three girls staring at Nikki and Jake from the cafeteria windows. They are probably deciding right now how they should vote and what they should say. My betrayal makes my throat feel tight. I swallow hard and look down at the ground. I will tell her. I'll explain and she'll understand. Eventually.

Raylene bounces up to the table, dragging Ross along by the hand. "We'll take two."

Evidently, they survived the scrutiny of Worthy and are still a couple. I realize I'm relieved.

"You have your tickets, right?" Max calls after me, but I pretend not to hear him. I go through the lunch line and pick up a sad-looking piece of pepperoni pizza.

If everything goes according to plan, I'll have a date to prom by this Friday night. But maybe I should wait and let Alex ask me in his own way?

No, I am definitely going to do it.

I take a seat by myself at the usual table, setting down my tray, but then see Taylor waving wildly at me from across the room.

"Over here, Linden!"

Jayla and Mia don't look up from the piles of lettuce and carrots in front of them, but Mia pushes her cheerleading pom-poms down on the bench and silently scoots over to make room for me. Jayla nods a greeting, and just like that, I fit in at the popular table, surrounded by the Lovelies. I know a lot of people in this cafeteria would kill to be in my shoes right now, but honestly, the view isn't any different.

"You should have gotten a salad," Mia tells Taylor, looking at her bagel. "Even an inch or two is going to be obvious in that mermaid dress you've picked out."

Taylor glares at her but pulls out all the middle of the half of bagel she's holding in her hand and takes a few tiny bites of the outside crust. I take a bite of my pizza and chew slowly. Looking down the table, I notice no one else has pizza. It's a mistake on my part. I put the slice down on my plate, my stomach growling in revolt.

Jayla finally makes eye contact with me. "I think your friend is so courageous."

Mia nods enthusiastically, flipping her long blonde braid over one shoulder. "A woman's worth should never be determined by how others feel about her. It's all about how you view yourself."

I'm pretty sure I saw this direct quote on Pinterest last week. Then I would have said Nikki was the living, breathing embodiment of this saying. Now I'm not so sure.

"Well, I know all about the inner strength it takes to be on Worthy," Taylor says, clutching her hand to her heart. "After all, I was on it *first*."

I do an inner eye roll. Sitting here is a bad idea. I should quit this publicity thing right now and go back to my comfortable table in the cheap seats of the cafeteria. But quitting in the middle of a plan has never been one of my strengths. Even if it's all going downhill fast.

"So what's up next, Linds?" Taylor says, turning to me. "We have to keep this prom momentum going."

Suddenly, I have a nickname from the Lovelies. As if it isn't weird enough to be sitting here.

"Prom is only two weeks away," I say. "Not a lot more time, but I'm thinking there should be one more really big promposal."

Mia makes a face. "Kind of last minute, don't you think?"

But Taylor isn't taking her bait. "Who?" she asks me.

I look everyone in the eye, up and down the table, my pulse racing. "Me."

"I didn't even know you were dating anyone," Jayla says.

"Well, I am." I take a breath in and announce, "I'm dating Alex Rivera."

It's the first time I've actually said it out loud, and my heart explodes with the thought of it.

Jayla just dips her forkful of lettuce into her oil-and-vinegar dressing and nods. Not exactly the reaction I was hoping for.

"Who is that?" Mia asks, and Jayla tells her, "He's on the baseball team."

"That cute catcher?" Mia asks, and Jayla nods; then Mia looks at me with her blue eyes all wide. "He's adorable," Mia says.

For a moment, I think she's going to jump up and do a little cheer just for me.

Jayla says, "I saw you sitting by him at the assembly, but I didn't know you were *dating.*"

"Well, we are," I say.

Taylor squeals and punches me in the arm. "This is going to be epic."

She seems even more enthusiastic after I explain the plan with the banner and the balloons.

"So romantic!" she cries.

"I know, right?" I'm excited by the enthusiastic reception, but a little overwhelmed.

Surprisingly, Jayla and Mia volunteer to help hold the sign at the game. "If we're all in the video, it will definitely have the most hits yet," Jayla says, obviously thinking about the potential for prom queen publicity.

"Is Nikki going to help?" Blair asks.

"I haven't talked to her about it." I deserve something to be about just me. If Nikki gets involved, everything will be about heart stickers and Worthy.

But before I can even try to explain, Taylor changes the subject. "What does your dress look like?" she asks between bagel nibbles.

I look up from my pizza. "I don't have one yet."

Taylor tilts her head to one side like she couldn't have possibly heard me correctly. "You're kidding, right?"

I shake my head. "I've been so busy with all the prom plans, I haven't really thought about it."

"We'll have to fix that." She gently pats me on the shoulder.

"Fix what?" Nikki is standing beside the table in her *Am I Good Enough?* shirt. She's clearly caught the tail end of our conversation.

Taylor takes a last long sip of her bottled water, then stands up. Everyone at the table quickly follows her lead, clearing trays and picking up trash.

"I have to get to class. I'll text you about dress shopping, Linds."

Nikki's eyebrows shoot up. "Seriously? You're going shopping with Taylor?"

"I didn't plan it. She just asked me right now." I don't know why I sound so defensive. "She's going to help with the promposal . . . " My voice trails off.

"You can't be serious. Why didn't you ask me?"

I feel like a traitor. "I wanted to ask you, but you've been so preoccupied with Worthy."

"So all of a sudden you're hanging out with your new 'friends'?" She makes air quotes with her fingers. Even though Nikki's always floated between different groups, I've never stretched myself this far.

Jealous, Nikki?

Her sarcasm makes me angry. Why wouldn't they be friends with me?

"You aren't the only one who is worthy," I say, surprised at the harshness in my tone.

Nikki puts her hands on her hips. "This is important,

Linden. We have to stand up for ourselves and let people know we can't be judged by the way we look. Worthy is my chance to do that in a big way."

But after our conversation last night, Nikki's words don't make sense to me. On one hand, she says looks don't matter. On the other, she keeps trying to change herself to make Jake like her more.

Which is it, Nikki?

Worthy has somehow twisted Nikki's confidence into a muddled mess, and now it's not only about proving her worth to everyone at school. It's also about Jake and how he makes her feel. I can't hold it back anymore. She has to know.

"You are worthy, Nikki. That's why I voted no." I blurt it out.

Nikki's mouth falls open, and I keep talking as fast as I can. "You deserve much more than someone like Jake. If I could have voted him unworthy, I would have."

Nikki shakes her head. "That's not fair. Of all people, I always thought you had my back."

My eyes fill up with tears. "I do," I whisper. "Always."

"But not now." Her words slice through me like the scissors she always keeps on her desk to cut through the fabric of her latest creations.

I have to explain. Tears spill out of my eyes and down my cheeks. I put my hands out, but she steps away from my reach. "I wanted you to see he wasn't right for you," I try to explain.

"That's my choice. Not yours." Her brown eyes are cold, her mouth tight. Now she has pinned me through the heart with guilt.

She's right and I'm so, so wrong. "I was trying to protect you," I mumble. "I didn't want you to be hurt."

"Don't you think I know what it feels like to not fit in? I don't *fit* anywhere. That's why I make my own place." She takes a step closer to me. "And some people appreciate that about me."

There is nothing more I can say. I watch her turn and walk away through the crowded hallway, and despite the swarms of pushing bodies all around me, I feel completely alone.

That night, I sit at my desk and think about everything that happened with Nikki. I love the power of words, but I just betrayed my best friend with only one.

No.

On the wall above me, judging me with all those empty squares, is my writing calendar. Three freaking stickers for the whole month? Who am I kidding? I have to accept it. I'm never going to break through this block if I can't trust someone enough to actually read what I write. Tears burn at my throat.

Murphy sniffs at my hand, drawing my attention away from my thoughts for a moment. I look down into his golden eyes and he puts his chin on my knee. My glance is encouraging, so he nudges me gently with his nose, pushing his soft chocolate snout underneath my hand. My fingers move ever so slightly, and Murphy snuggles in deeper, positioning my hand perfectly on top of his head for stroking. The response is almost automatic. My fingers relax into his fur. All of this emotion has to be good for something. Finally, I turn back to my computer. I write a while and cry a while. It is the perfect combination.

Congratulations, Nikki!

72% say YES!

You are WORTHY!

Hey, Hornets! Wake up tomorrow, roll out of bed, and start judging. Someone new will be under the WORTHY microscope!

CHAPTER SIXTEEN

On Monday, I stand in front of my closet, my mind still clouded with sleep, staring at the rows of clothes. I could put that skirt with that top, but what shoes? Or those sneakers with that pair of jeans, but what else? Nikki would know, but she didn't answer my texts all weekend. I deserve her silence.

Picking out my outfit is way too difficult, so I give up and focus on putting makeup on instead, trying to cover up the puffiness from last night's cry-fest. My favorite NARS concealer covers the dark circles pretty well, but does nothing to hide the guilt looking back at me from the mirror. My hair is a tangled mess and I don't have the energy to tame it into some kind of style, so I just twist it into a long, low braid. I add a quick coat of mascara and some chocolate-brown shadow, then call it done. No contacts today. My glasses will just add one small buffer between me and the world.

I'm glad Nikki was voted worthy, but somehow it makes what I did even worse. I should have supported her or, better yet, not let myself be dragged into Worthy at all.

When I finally turn on my phone, it goes crazy with notifications. There are no texts from Nikki, but a bunch from Taylor.

TAYLOR: OMG

TAYLOR: HELLO?

TAYLOR: YOU'VE SEEN IT RIGHT??

TAYLOR: CHECK WORTHY

I refuse to be sucked into this again. I'm done with Worthy. And, just to cement the deal, I put down my phone. I open my desk drawer and take out a sheet of stickers. Peeling a bright pink sticker off the top, I stick it carefully to my writing calendar on top of yesterday's date. I step back. It's a start. I actually got work done last night. I give a contented sigh.

My phone buzzes again and I look down.

TAYLOR: NOW!

I turn my phone facedown on my nightstand. Then I go to the closet and pick my clothes out—a pale pink tunic sweater and some print leggings. I look at the rows of shoes. Black motorcycle boots? Seems appropriate for my mood. I pull them out, but before I can put them on, my phone buzzes again.

ALEX: HANG IN THERE. THIS WILL ALL DIE DOWN SOON

I frown. I put one boot on, lace it up, then leave the other one lying on the floor to text him back.

ME: WHAT ARE YOU TALKING ABOUT?

I hit send, then pull on the other boot. But before I tie

the laces, my phone goes crazy. I've never had this many texts before eight o'clock in the morning. A feeling of dread pushes into my sleepy brain and I grab my phone again.

ALEX: CHECK OUT WORTHY BUT DON'T FREAK

TAYLOR: LINDS, ARE YOU THERE? HAVE YOU SEEN IT?????

My heart starts to pound. Finally, I open Worthy. My face stares back up at me.

Right next to Alex's.

It's a picture of us that I posted on Instagram, a selfie. I'm hugging him from behind and we're laughing.

I'm on Worthy.

For a long moment I just go blank. My hand holding the phone starts to shake.

No. No. No. No.

My mind is racing and there is suddenly a sharp, horrible pain throbbing behind my right eye.

I've been flung onto the crazy Worthy stage and the curtain has been stripped away, leaving me exposed for the whole world to see. To discuss. To judge.

The comments are already piling up on the screen in front of me like writhing snakes full of poison. I imagine them as lime green with razor-sharp fangs. They twist and curl around my skull, hissing their venom deep into my eardrums.

Ssss-see? Sssss-seeee?

She's cute, but not his type. Too serious and too quiet.

Give me a break. These two together?? I don't see it.

Tears sting in my eyes. It's as if I've been punched by the words scrolling down the screen. I drop the phone onto my bed and take a step away, but it is too late. The messages are already slithering in behind my eyes and into the darkest corners of my brain. People don't like me. It makes me feel sad and a little sick to my stomach.

I grab for my phone to call Nikki, but then remember we aren't talking. Nikki is one of the few people who knows how all this scrutiny feels. She could tell me exactly how to face all the attention. When she was on Worthy, she sashayed her way into the school, cutting a wide path for me to follow. Just like always. But Worthy has ruined that relationship, too.

I stare down at my phone, wondering what would happen if I texted her and said I'm sorry. But what if she doesn't answer? And why hasn't she texted or called *me*?

I turn off my phone again and put it in my bag.

I won't go to school. I'll tell my parents I'm sick. It wouldn't really be a lie because my stomach is churning and my hands are trembling. I can't stay in my room forever, but maybe I can stay here long enough that Worthy moves on to someone else.

"Linden!" My dad is calling up the stairs. "Someone's at the door for you."

Oh my God. I can't ignore my dad. I have to say something. The roaring in my ears is so loud I can hardly think, but I walk to the top of the stairs and look down.

"Who is it?" I call.

But I can already see who it is. Alex is standing in the entryway, looking up the steps at me, his face all drawn and serious.

"I thought you might want a ride to school," he says. His eyes lock on mine, and I nod.

I'm grateful Alex manages the small talk with my dad and even greets Rat, like absolutely nothing is up. Staying home from school is not an option now, so I follow Alex out the door and down the driveway to his car. When we get in, Alex puts both hands on the wheel and stares straight ahead. He doesn't start the car.

"I tried to call you before I came over," he says.

"I turned off my phone."

"Good." He still doesn't look at me.

"Why me?" I ask, pressing my hands to my cheeks. I'm trying so hard not to cry.

He turns to face me, putting both hands on my shoulders. "Look at me, Linden."

I pull my hands away from my face, biting my lip to keep the emotion inside.

"I don't know why they picked us," he says. "If I could fix it, I would. Please don't cry."

I nod, numb. I like that he said *us*. It reminds me that I'm not in this alone. He cups my cheek in his hand, wiping away a tear from the corner of my eye with one finger. In spite of everything, I smile. He runs a thumb along my bottom lip. Slowly. Then he leans in to kiss me—very softly—following along the line his thumb traced with his lips.

I wish we could stay here longer, but he turns back to the steering wheel and starts the car. "I have to be out at the baseball field for practice this morning, so I can't go in with you," he says, putting the car in drive and pulling away from the curb, "but we can eat lunch together."

"You always eat in the weight room with the other baseball players."

"Not today," he says.

Alex drops me off at the door. Before I get out, he holds up three fingers. "Keep your head up," he says.

"What is that?"

"The *Hunger Games* salute," he says, with a grin. "Mrs. Pirtle recommended it to me on Facebook. Good book."

My laugh is a little wobbly. Before I slam the door, I hear him shout, "And stay off that app."

I drag myself through the front door just before the morning bell. Two girls stand by the doors to the band hall, whispering and pointing. At me. Of course. I take the hall down by the main office to try to avoid the usual crowd. My stomach is still doing something crazy, but I try to ignore it. Spending the morning in the bathroom throwing up is not an option.

I hurry past the senior row of lockers, praying no one sees me. It is pretty quiet, not too many kids milling around, but there are still glances and nudges as I pass.

Not a good sign. The final steps to the door of my first-period class stretch out endlessly. My legs feel like logs. There is no avoiding it. I have to go through that doorway and face the rows of judgment on the other side. Stopping for a minute one step away, I take one deep breath in and then let it out slowly.

I force myself to walk into the room. Rows of heads swivel my way. A frozen moment, then the heads huddle together in groups, whispering and shooting glances my way as they deliberate my fate. I walk down the aisle to my desk, feeling the flush rise up in my neck. Slipping into my chair, I try to make myself invisible, but it isn't working.

Taylor sits across the room with one long leg draped over the other, her toe tapping restlessly against the floor. She catches me looking at her and mouths the word "Sorry." I feel my shoulders slump. I'm an object of pity. I look back down at my notebook, but I still feel her eyes on me. I feel everyone watching me. My fingers twitch to get my phone out of my bag and check my standing on Worthy, but I can't imagine anything worse. Still, I slide my hand into my bag and click on my phone.

The bell rings and everyone gets quiet—or at least quieter—with conversations moving into sneaking whispers and sideway glances. If I keep my eyes trained on my notebook and scribble quickly, maybe I can blend into my chair. The teacher starts the lesson. I glance up from the notebook and nod once in a while, like I am interested, but

I really have no idea what's being said. I could cry or yell or crumple into a huddle in front of them all, but everyone would just talk about my breakdown for the rest of the year. They would love that. I grit my teeth and straighten up, staring down two whispering girls in the row beside me. They giggle nervously, but turn away. One small victory.

When the bell finally rings, students rush out the door to the hallway, squealing, yelling, and laughing. I throw my backpack over one shoulder and take the stairs two at a time. I slam open the door on the first floor and run directly into Taylor on the other side.

"Whoa," she says, reaching out to steady me with both hands as the door swings shut behind me. I keep walking, but she follows me to my locker.

"How's it going?" she asks.

"Great. Just great," I mutter, opening my locker door.

"You're sure you are okay? You don't look so good."

I shake my head. "Thanks a lot."

"Listen." She tosses her perfectly curled blonde hair over one shoulder. "There's no such thing as bad publicity."

I pull out my history book and slam my locker.

"Don't let this stuff bother you."

"That's easy for you to say. You were worthy."

"You'll be fine without Alex."

Now she has my attention. I turn and face her. "What are you talking about?" I ask.

"I just mean, if it turns out you guys weren't meant to be . . . " She trails off with a shrug.

"Being on Worthy isn't changing anything with me and Alex," I tell her. "I'm still asking him to the prom."

She bites one pink, pouty lip with her impossibly white teeth. I notice the front incisor has a tiny chip on one side. Not so perfect after all. "Are you sure?" she asks. "Maybe you should wait and see how it all turns out."

Anger hits me then. I walk away down the hall. "I'm not waiting on anything," I say over my shoulder.

"You're right," Taylor says quickly, racing to catch up with me. "It doesn't matter what people say."

But it does.

That realization creeps in so silently, I am unable to recognize it until it is already rooted and growing wildly through my heart. I stop suddenly in the middle of the hall, and Taylor bumps into my back.

"What are they saying about me?" I turn around, crossing my arms and steeling my heart.

"The voting is going pretty well," Taylor says. "*Some* people are saying good things. It's just that Alex is getting a lot of attention these days with the baseball team doing so well, so it just makes it that much harder for you to be . . . " She pauses, then says a little quieter, "Worthy."

I look away, down at the floor, and then glance back up at her face. She tilts her head, smiling ever so slightly. "Rule number one. Don't read the comments. Ever."

She's right. Nobody really wants someone to sit down and tell them all the things they dislike about you. And there could be a million things. It could be something stupid, like that my legs are too short. Or because I got a better math grade than they did once on a test in fifth grade. Or that I wear red too much.

What could I do to prove I deserve to date Alex?

And if it's something I can't change? This face? This body? Myself? My self? Tell me. What do I do then?

Right before lunch, I find Alex at his locker.

"I can't take it," I groan, coming up to him.

The inside of his locker is evidently fascinating, because he doesn't look at me, instead staring straight ahead at a stack of books and a discarded red hoodie.

He shrugs, then slams the locker door shut. A muscle twitches along his jawline. Finally, he turns to face me. "Linden, I told you this is stupid. I don't care what other people think about us."

It shouldn't matter to me either. I want to believe I am stronger than that. It is such a demeaning realization, because it means I know I'm not. I feel like such a coward.

"Can we just forget about it?" Alex asks.

I wish I could, but I'm too aware it's happening and I've been sucked in way too far.

I stare at him, trying to see if he is hiding something or if he thinks differently about me now. If he is pretending so he won't hurt my feelings, I can't tell. A growing crowd watches us, like sharks gathering for blood in the water. Then my phone buzzes and I look down, my stomach churning. The phone slips out of my shaking hand, but I scramble to retrieve it off the floor before the buzzing stops. Alex takes it out of my hand before I can read anything on the screen.

"All you have to do is turn it off." He clicks the phone to black. "See?"

He slides the phone into my bag, but I know Worthy is still there waiting. Everyone is still talking about us, watching us, and the votes are pouring in even as we stand there.

What if I'm not worthy?

"What's for lunch?" Alex's question brings my attention back to him. He smiles at me and I can't help but smile back. Just a little bit. I tuck my hair behind my ear and pull out a brown paper bag from my backpack.

"Peanut butter and banana sandwiches?" I shrug.

"Sounds perfect," he says.

I look around. "You don't have to eat lunch," I say, then add, "with me."

"I want to eat lunch with *you*," Alex says. I know he is trying to make me feel better. He's a good guy. Too good for me? "And today we're eating in the courtyard. It's a perfect day to be outside."

Outside in the courtyard, the sun is so hot that the air I suck in and out feels like it is scalding the inside of my throat. The sweater I chose to wear was definitely the wrong choice. I feel a small trickle of sweat running down my back between my shoulder blades.

At first, we eat in silence, but I'm really just pretending to eat. The idea of swallowing even a small bite makes me nauseous. I was crazy to think I could handle this kind of attention. Every movement I make feels awkward and exaggerated. I can almost hear the whispers.

She's too girly. She's not girly enough. She's too smart. She's not smart enough. She's just not . . . ENOUGH.

There are several kids watching, a few taking pictures. I see Nikki inside sitting at our usual lunch table, but she is the only one not looking my way. I miss her. All I want is to crawl back into her shadow and stare at people's shoes.

Alex finishes the last bite of the peanut butter sandwich and wipes the crumbs off his mouth with the paper towel.

"You should talk to her."

Of course he noticed Nikki and I weren't speaking. We've been inseparable for as long as anyone can remember, so it's pretty strange to see one of us without the other.

I try to keep my voice light. "She doesn't want to talk to me."

"Have you even tried?"

I look down at my motorcycle boots. "I'm sorry. Everything is such a mess . . . " My mouth goes dry and I fight to keep my voice even. "Why do you want to be with me, Alex?"

Alex frowns, hurt darkening his face. "Because I like you. And some stupid app isn't going to change that."

But you could do better. Everyone is saying it.

I look over his shoulder to see two boys walking by, laughing and looking toward me. I feel my face burn. I remember how I once thought of Worthy as a magnifying glass, lighting the student body on fire. And I am right in the middle of the blaze, with no hope of escape.

Linden Wilson & Alex Rivera

<u>IS SHE WORTHY?</u>

Here's what you are saying:

* Talk about a snob! She doesn't speak to anyone if she can help it.

* He's a rising star and she is not.

* Pretty, smart, talented. Of course she's worthy!

* He could definitely do better.

The vote is in . . .

Stay tuned . . .

CHAPTER SEVENTEEN

It's the last period on Thursday and ten minutes until I can escape the side eyes and gossip. When Alex and I went up on Worthy, I didn't think things could get any worse. But today the vote will be announced, and this is definitely worse.

Nikki called last night, but I didn't answer the phone. Now that I'm the one in the hot seat, I feel even guiltier for what I did to her on Worthy. I tried to catch her eye this morning in class and later in the hall, but she never looked my way. I wasn't brave enough to walk right up to her and start talking. *What would I say?*

Everyone is sneaking peeks at their phones and I'm completely paranoid, thinking every time someone says anything, they're talking about me. Mr. Landmann has given up on keeping our attention right up until the bell, so everyone is chatting in clumps while he grades homework at his desk.

I sit with my hands clenched and my nails digging into my palms until my phone buzzes in my bag. Maybe this is it. The vote is in. I feel myself starting to sweat. I carefully slide my phone out and hide it in my lap under the desk. I glance down quickly, but it's not Worthy.

ALEX: THINKING ABOUT YOU! COULDN'T FIND AN EMOJI FOR HUNGER GAMES SALUTE.

My lips twitch into a tiny smile. I look up from my phone and take a deep breath. This is all going to go away.

Taylor stretches her long arms out over her expensively streaked blonde hair and sighs. "This Worthy thing has become such a distraction from all things prom," she groans.

"It's just so random," Jayla says, looking over at me. "I don't get what makes someone worthy to even *be* on that thing."

Mia giggles like this is the funniest thing ever. I want to smack her.

Somehow I need to stop all the talk about Worthy. If only for a moment, to catch my breath and calm my shaking hands.

"So you are all in for my promposal tomorrow at the game, right?" I ask.

Jayla's mouth drops open. "You're still going ahead with it?"

"Why wouldn't I?" I try to look defiant. I gulp down my anxiety. This is the best way to show everyone that I'm perfect for Alex and that Alex is perfect for me.

Taylor's eyebrows shoot up in surprise, but she is the first one to recover. Leaning across the aisle, she pats me on my knee like some kind of grandmother. "Oh, sweetie, I think that is so brave of you. Of course we'll be there. Won't we?"

She glances over at Mia, who looks back and forth at both of us, obviously confused.

"Oh, come on," Taylor says. "It'll be fun."

Mia smiles, but it's insincere. "Sure. I'll be there."

"I wouldn't miss it for the world," Jayla says.

My eyes drop to the phone in my lap. I've tried to keep from looking, but the promise of a final vote sucks me in like quicksand. Anxious flutters erupt in my stomach.

I open the app.

The result is in.

"Oh my God, oh my God, oh my God." My words are jerky, my breath ragged. I don't even realize I'm saying it out loud. Everyone turns around in their desks to stare, and Mr. Landmann looks up from his desk and lowers his reading glasses. My eyes squeeze tight, as though I can make the words on the screen disappear.

"What is wrong with you?" Taylor hisses at me.

I open my eyes and stare back at her. I feel dizzy. Actually light-headed.

"What is it?" Taylor asks.

"I'm not worthy," I whisper.

So sorry, Linden!

58% say NO!

You are NOT WORTHY!

CHAPTER EIGHTEEN

I don't remember much after that. I get home somehow, but it is mostly a blur. Mom is at the firehouse. Dad and Rat are going out to dinner and a movie.

"Do you want to come?" Rat asks. "It's a dystopian Romeo and Juliet story. With a computer-controlled apocalypse. And anime, of course."

"I can't imagine why Ever doesn't want to go to something like that." My dad grins at me, pulling on his jacket, but I don't smile back.

Instead, I shake my head. "No, I'll just make something here for dinner."

"Are you feeling okay?" Dad puts a hand on my forehead.

"Just a headache," I say. "I'll be fine after I take some aspirin."

Dad kisses me on the forehead and they both head out the door, arguing about the best anime movie of all time.

Later, I sit at the dining room table that seats four, staring at my dinner of macaroni and cheese. Usually, macaroni and cheese feels like warm spoonfuls of comfort, but nothing is helping me feel better tonight. The blinds on the small dining room window are pulled up, and in between small bites, I watch the neighbors on the small tree-shaded street, out enjoying the mild March evening. Alex is at baseball practice now, but he'll come home to a table full of quinceañera plans. Nikki is probably arguing with Maricel about something. I should call her, but all the words are tumbling around in my brain with no way out. I have no idea what I could say to make her or myself feel any better.

I take a few more bites, but leave the rest uneaten.

Upstairs, I take a shower, standing under the hot water for a long time, and try to sort out how I'm feeling. Mostly I'm just angry that I care. About everything.

When I finally get out, I take out my contacts, pull my hair up into a messy pony, and put on some sweats and a tank top. My phone buzzes with a text and I so want to ignore it. But I don't.

ALEX: COME TO THE WINDOW.

When I pull up the blinds and look down, he's standing there at the curb, looking up at me. He must have just come from practice because his hair is all spiky from sweat and he looks like he's been rolling around in the dirt. My heart melts.

He holds up his phone and points to it. My phone immediately starts to ring. When I answer it, Alex asks, "You okay?"

"Yes," I say, because just seeing him out there on my lawn makes me feel better than I have all day. "Why didn't you come to the door?"

"I'm a mess. Besides, I'm already late. I'm supposed to be at some dance practice for Izzy's party." He clears his throat. "But I wanted to see you."

I smile into the phone. "You're crazy."

"And I wanted to tell you that Worthy doesn't matter."

"Okay," I say quietly, pressing a hand against the windowpane.

He lifts his hand in response. "I have to go. I'll call you later?"

When I hang up, I watch his car drive away with my forehead pressed against the window and my fingers still spread out on the glass in a silent good-bye.

I finally turn away from the window and flop down on my bed, staring up at the ceiling. Alex is right. Worthy doesn't matter, and I'm going to prove it by going ahead with my promposal plan tomorrow at the baseball game. Going to prom together is only the beginning. There will be many, many more magical evenings to come.

Or at least I hope there will be.

CHAPTER NINETEEN

On Friday afternoon I watch Alex step into the batter's box. The chatter from the infielders and from the team in the dugout is loud and conflicting.

"Come on, Alex!" one of his teammates calls from the dugout. "You can do it."

"Watch the ball!" another yells.

The catcher tries to confuse Alex. "Hey batter, batter."

All this noise and excitement is the best thing I can do to distract me from the Worthy decree. Besides, none of it is going to matter when I pull off the biggest promposal yet and everyone has to eat their words just one day after the verdict was posted.

I look around nervously, but everyone is watching Alex. Not me. I gulp down my insecurities and set my jaw. *Yes.* I'm going through with my plan.

I catch sight of Nikki down near the bottom of the stands. She looks around at the same time and our eyes meet. In that moment I remember years ago when Nikki told me Martin Wells had kissed her behind the tree outside the playground. We pinkie swore to always tell each other our secrets. If I went down there now, maybe we could fix this. But it feels like sending a note in grade school that reads, "Do you want to be my friend? Circle yes or no."

What if she says no?

Just then, Jake pushes his way through the crowd to Nikki's side. He puts his arm around her and pulls her into his chest. I look away. This isn't the right time to talk to Nikki. Not with Jake there.

Alex steps out of the batter's box and takes a couple of deep breaths. I can tell he's nervous, but not nearly as nervous as me. I take a breath. It is bottom of the ninth and just half an inning away from my chance at redemption.

Alex taps the dirt, repositions his fingers on the tape. When he steps back into the box, he looks the pitcher in the eye. The ball comes in at rocket speed, a little high, but he swings at it, and everyone can hear the unmistakable sound of the bat connecting to the sweet spot. The crowd goes wild and Alex rounds the bases to the sound of the cheering. I jump up and down, yelling like a banshee.

That's my boyfriend and in a few minutes you are all going to know it.

The noise is deafening, but Taylor cups her hands over her mouth and shouts in my ear. "He's really good."

I nod, grinning widely and clutching the rolled-up paper banner in my hand. Everyone showed up as promised. I'm nervous, excited, and so freaking scared.

The game is over and the home team wins once again. Everyone is congratulating Alex out on the field. It's go time for my promposal team. My pulse is pounding like horses galloping through my body. Alex looks up at the bleachers and sees me. He waves, smiling. The pump of the adrenaline is there, pounding into my muscles and up my spine, but now it is mingled with confidence. I was right to go ahead with the plan.

Taylor, Mia, Blair, Jayla, and I set up down by the backstop in front of the still-crowded bleachers. The news has spread, and a large group of students gathers behind us, waiting for the action.

"Good luck, Linden!" someone yells, and someone else laughs, but it isn't about luck. It's about not looking at the ground anymore. It's about doing something outrageous and public. Something I've never had the courage to do before. In this moment, I feel capable of this and so much more. The thought of it all has my pulse pounding again, my smile growing until it takes over my face.

Breathe. Just breathe.

With all my being, I focus on unrolling the paper and not on the buzz building inside my stomach. Jayla and Blair take their places at each end of the banner, and Taylor carefully removes the red and green helium balloons from their hiding places inside a plastic trash bag. Mia positions herself for the best angles with her phone ready to shoot the video that will go out in every possible form within minutes of the answer.

ALEX RIVERA, WILL YOU GO TO PROM WITH ME? the banner reads.

Alex trots off the field and through the gate. I hold a balloon in each hand, waiting with this goofy grin on my face. Alex's brow wrinkles in confusion when he sees the sign; then it slowly registers. He stops in front of me.

"What are you doing, Linden?" he asks.

"I know we haven't talked about it yet, but . . . "

"Don't . . . " He shakes his head.

"You're supposed to choose a balloon," Mia yells excitedly from behind her phone.

"Are you getting all of this?" Taylor asks her.

Alex isn't smiling. "Let's not do this now," he says.

I can barely hear him. Then he leans in to say in my ear, "Can I talk to you privately?"

But nothing about this plan is private. "Sure," I say. "Just pick the balloon."

I hold out the green one to make it easy and smile into the camera.

"I can't go to prom with you, Linden."

"What?" There's too much noise. I must have heard him wrong.

He reaches out and takes the red balloon from me. "I can't." He's dead serious.

I freeze, taking it in, but not saying anything at first. My fingers open and the green balloon floats up and away.

My eyes fill up with tears and everything goes blurry. Alex sees the look on my face. "Wait. Don't freak out. I can explain."

It is too late. I thought he thought the app was stupid. But he does think Worthy is right. I'm not good enough for him.

Taylor gasps. "Oh. My. God."

She turns to speak directly into Mia's phone like she is a reporter at the scene. "He said no."

CHAPTER TWENTY

Backing out of the parking lot, I catch sight of my face in the rearview mirror. My eyes are wild. Like crazy. And my jaw is clenched so tight there is a muscle pulsing in my cheek.

This isn't the way it was supposed to go.

My phone starts to buzz. It's Alex, but I don't answer. Instead, I turn off my phone and stuff it down into my bag.

I get home. When I walk into the house, Mom is sitting on the couch waiting.

"Can we talk for a second?" she asks me when I walk through the door. "Come sit down."

"Please, not now, Mom." I keep walking toward the stairs. "I have a ton of homework."

"I saw the video," she says quietly.

It's already online?

My heart plunges toward my feet and shock floods through my body. I can feel the tears coming, but I swallow them back down. "How?"

"I saw Max outside when I came home. He told me."

She pats the empty spot beside her on the couch and I sit down next to her, sighing heavily. Tears are running down my face continuously, but I'm not making any noise.

"Linden," my mom says, like you say to a hurt animal to calm it down. "You're going to be okay."

"I'm not okay."

"Not now, but you will be."

She holds out her arms. I lean in and she pulls me close. That's when I start to sob—big, ugly, gulping gasps.

When I can finally talk, I say, "I had a plan, but it all went wrong. And Alex and I were on this app called Worthy . . . "

"Max told me." She wraps her arms around my shoulders and looks into my eyes. "It's a stupid game. They'll move on to someone else soon. That's how these things work. Just ignore it."

"I wish I could. People are saying Alex and I don't go together." I gulp in air, trying to talk through my tears. "But I like him a lot and Worthy has ruined everything."

"You can't fix what other people think," Mom says.

Tears roll down my cheeks. "I wish I were as strong as you," I say.

"Nobody's perfect," she says. "Especially me. I've been so caught up with this new job."

She looks so guilty, I instantly feel sorry for her. "You had a lot on your mind."

"That's no excuse." She takes my hand and holds it in hers. "Don't live your life based on other people's judgments, Linden. It will just end up making you miserable long after this silly app fades away."

Mom pulls me into her side and we sit like that a moment in silence. Finally, she says, "You can still go to the prom, you know."

I shake my head. "No, I can't. But it's just one night. No big deal." I'm lying and we both know it.

"But it's *prom*." She says it like it is heaven or something. I'm surprised. Mom's never cared much about dances and dressing up. "Everyone wants to go to prom." She pauses, a smile growing on her face. "I went with your father when we were seniors in high school."

"And it was magical . . . " I say, rolling my eyes just to tease her.

"No, it was horrible." She shudders dramatically. "He had a bad reaction to the lobster we ate. He'd been saving up to take me to that restaurant for months, and it just ended up with him throwing up all over my shoes in the parking lot."

I laugh. I've never heard that story before.

Mom pats my hand in her lap. "I'm sorry if I've been so crazy about recipes and the new job and . . . everything. I haven't been paying enough attention to you." Her voice breaks, and I feel a lump in my throat. "You mean everything to me."

My body relaxes, and I give her a watery smile. "I know that, Mom."

With her other hand she touches my cheek. Then she

says, "Go get cleaned up for dinner. You're a mess." And we both laugh.

Murphy follows me upstairs and jumps onto the bed, his brown eyes watching me as I stalk back and forth across my room. I stop at the window and look down at the front yard, where Alex stood talking to me on the phone. Back before I made a fool of myself in front of the whole school. The tears return. I blink them away, angrily.

"I have to pull myself together," I mutter under my breath, and Murphy's tail thumps against my bedspread. I sit down on the bed beside him and rub his soft brown ears. He rolls over on his back so I can reach his tummy. "It's not like we were dating that long," I tell him, but I know I'm just trying to convince myself. "It just wasn't meant to be."

If I keep saying it out loud, maybe I will start to believe it. I shift back against my headboard, push my earbuds into my ears, and turn up my saddest playlist to full volume. I pull my journal out of my nightstand and start to write, the words pouring out on the page.

The internet creates beasts who don't have the nerve to say anything to your face, but speak their poison in typed messages behind computer screens. There is no beauty hiding there, and the ugliness is so much more than skin deep.

My pen stops moving and I stare down at the words I wrote. I wonder what Alex would think if he read them, but I know he'll never get the chance. I scribble more words on the page.

Regret. Pain. Heartrending.

I almost jump out of my skin when Dad suddenly appears in my line of sight, interrupting the music pounding into my brain.

"You're supposed to knock," I say, after I remove one earbud.

"I did. You didn't hear me." He taps the top of my head for emphasis.

"What's up?" I ask.

"There's someone here for you."

I remove the other earbud. "Who?"

"It's Alex. He said he wants to talk to you."

I chew on my lip. "Tell him I'm not here."

He shakes his head. "He knows you're here, Linden. I told him I would come up and get you."

When I get downstairs, Alex is standing inside our foyer, his brows knit together. I take a deep breath and close my eyes, preparing myself for the unavoidable conversation. When I open my eyes, he's still standing there with this sad smile on his face.

"Why haven't you been answering your phone?"

I lie. "My battery is dead."

"Can we talk?" I nod, and he opens the front door. "Out here?"

I follow him out to the front steps and sit down. Alex sighs heavily. "I wanted to explain about this afternoon."

"You don't have to explain," I whisper, biting my lip and bracing myself for what's going to come. I try to control my voice, making it sound like I'm not about to cry. "I guess Worthy was right after all. We don't belong together."

"Nobody belongs to anyone," Alex says.

Neither of us says anything for a moment. My fingers are itching to reach out and touch him, but his eyes are so sad. This is the part of the movie where a breakup song would start playing. But there is no soundtrack. No canned laughter. No happy ending.

He finally speaks. "My sister's quinceañera is the same night as the prom. That's why I can't go with you."

I blink at him, not sure I heard him right. He's not breaking up with me.

"I was going to ask you to go with me, but I didn't want you to miss out on the prom. I know how hard you've worked on it."

Relief floods over me. "I thought the verdict made you think . . . differently about me." My voice breaks.

"I told you I didn't care about Worthy." He's scrutinizing me, his long, dark lashes flickering as his eyes search my face.

"I know. I'm sorry." I misjudged him. "But everyone thinks . . . "

"Forget it," Alex says. "It doesn't matter what everybody thinks." I look at him, trying to discern whether he is being truthful. His eyes are steady on mine and he doesn't look away. "You're important to me, but so is my family."

"I wasn't trying to make you choose," I say. "But if we could just explain to the people at school that you didn't say no because of Worthy . . . "

"It's none of their business."

So you're not going to do anything? Are you ashamed of me?

"Evidently, it's everyone's business now," I say. "The video of my promposal is being posted and shared everywhere. It's validating everyone's vote on Worthy. It's humiliating. Have you seen it?"

"No, I haven't, and I'm not going to look. Whatever's between us has nothing to do with everyone else, and nothing to do with some video online," he says.

"The thing is," I start to say, then stop. "Maybe we could film a little explanation or something?"

He turns to face me, reaching out to put his hands on my shoulders and staring directly into my eyes. "It doesn't matter to me what other people think, Linden. Why is that so hard for you to believe?"

But I can't give up. I stepped out of my comfortable shadow in a big way with this promposal. He could step up, too. "Or you could leave the quinceañera a little early and we could go to prom later?" I offer. "That way you could go to both." There's a long silence, and I know what he's going to say.

Alex shakes his head. "I'm sorry, Linden. You know I can't do that."

I glance away from the intensity of his stare. I can't look

at him looking at me anymore. *If he really cared about me, wouldn't he want to fix things?*

"Evidently, this Worthy decree matters to *you*," he says finally. "A lot."

"It's not that . . . " My voice trails off, and I realize I have no idea what to say next.

It does matter. The thought makes my heart hurt.

"You're not going to do *anything*?" I whisper.

"To fight Worthy?"

To stand up for me.

I nod.

He shakes his head.

"Maybe this isn't such a good idea," I say quietly.

"What?"

"Us," I say. "Maybe we aren't right for each other."

Quietly, he asks, "Do you really believe that?"

I don't. But everyone else does.

He stands up. "Are you going to write down how it feels to break someone's heart? I think that'd make a great story."

My heart stops. I broke his heart? Me?

"I'll see you around, Linden," Alex says, and now my heart doesn't just hurt—it shatters into a million different slivers of glass. But I don't say anything and he walks away, back straight and never slowing down.

I turn to go inside, not wanting to watch him leave. When I am sure he must be gone, I lean in to rest my forehead on the door and close my eyes.

CHAPTER TWENTY-ONE

The next morning is Saturday, and even though I have to go work at the library, at least there is no school. It's the only thing that gets me out of bed. The thought of walking through the halls after Friday night's fiasco at the ball field is bad enough, but I know seeing Alex will be even worse.

If things could get worse.

When I turn on my phone, I can't help but check Worthy. There have been no new posts since I was deemed unworthy.

There are no messages from Alex.

But there are two missed calls from Nikki, and three texts.

NIKKI: HOW ARE YOU?

Then, an hour later: **HELLO? ARE YOU THERE?**

Finally: **I MISS YOU.**

I miss her, too. So much. But I'm not ready to write back yet.

That afternoon, I help Mrs. Pirtle Skype with her grandson, Justin, a young marine in a camouflage uniform. He is standing in front of a Humvee.

"How are the treatments going?" Justin asks. I look over at Mrs. Pirtle. Today she's wearing a tulip-covered scarf to cover her bald head. The red flowers are a stark contrast to the paleness of her skin, but her eyes are bright with excitement as she leans in to see the computer screen.

"Dr. Patterson told me there are little soldiers inside the chemo. So when they put them in your body they have to fight real hard to kill off the cancer. All that fighting inside is why I feel so bad right now."

The young marine laughs. "Just close your eyes and imagine them blowing up all those cancer cells. I'll help." He closes his eyes and makes loud explosion noises.

Mrs. Pirtle smiles weakly, then closes her eyes, too. Suddenly, there is the noise of engines starting up and yelling in the background. Justin looks offscreen. "I'm going to have to go now. Don't worry about me, Grams. I'll be fine."

"Promise?" Mrs. Pirtle asks.

"Absolutely. You just concentrate on blowing up those cancer cells." He looks offscreen again: "I have to go for now. I love you and I'll be home soon."

His hand is raised to wave good-bye when his side of screen goes black.

"Stay safe," Mrs. Pirtle whispers. Her open hand moves to touch the screen, then she wipes away tears from her eyes.

I'm struck by how much power there is to hurt and heal within that screen.

Afterward, I sit cross-legged on the carpet in between the shelves of books, trying to soak up their comfort. I'm rereading *Graceling* to channel all of Katsa's strength. But I know none of the stories would feature someone like me. I'm definitely not hero material. For once, being surrounded by books only makes me feel worse. I screwed everything up.

My eyes shift away from the shelves. Kat stands at the end of the aisle with her hands on her hips. Her curvy body is silhouetted from the window behind her. I'm sure she's there to scold me about escaping from the front desk, but instead she comes down the aisle and sits on the floor beside me.

Evidently, even Kat Lee feels sorry for me. I must have hit the bottom of the barrel.

"Did you know I have an older brother?" she asks, and I shake my head. It's a random question.

"He had a hard time in school. People bullied him online a lot."

"I'm sorry," I say, and I am, because now I know how that feels.

"He tried to commit suicide."

The air is sucked out of my lungs. I'm not prepared for this. "I didn't know."

"Not many people did. He's better now. In college. Doing well." She slides back on the carpet until she can rest against the shelf behind her. "I tried to get back at the guy who started it all, but I didn't handle it well."

This must have been the incident that brought her to the library for community service.

I swallow hard. Guilt swells in my chest. I've been so selfish. I'm not the only one with problems. Some people, like Mrs. Pirtle and Kat, are dealing with things even worse than I could imagine. "I'm sorry."

"Yeah. It's different when it's personal." Kat looks over at me. "What I'm trying to say is, you can't fight it the way I did, but you can fight."

"How? I don't know how to stop that stupid app."

Kat shakes her head. "The app isn't the problem. I could take that down in minutes, but something else would just take its place."

Kat could destroy Worthy? The thought is intriguing.

"I just want someone to tell me what to do." I'm not only thinking about Worthy. I'm thinking about Alex, too. A lot.

Kat says, "You'll have to figure that out for yourself."

I'm leaving the library when I get a text from Taylor.

TAYLOR: CRISIS AVERTED. WOLF INVITED ME TO PROM. STILL ON FOR AWARD CEREMONY?

ME: NOT GOING TO PROM

TAYLOR: YOU HAVE TO GO!

ME: NO

TAYLOR: MEET ME AT MALL TONIGHT. HAVE TO PICK UP GIFT CERTIFICATES FOR CONTEST.

ME: NO

TAYLOR: THIS IS YOUR RESPONSIBILITY!!!! YOU CAN'T LET US DOWN NOW.

ME: FINE. I'LL BE THERE.

"Where's Mia and Jayla?" I ask Taylor when I catch up with her outside Nordstrom.

"Mia had cheerleading practice and Jayla"—Taylor pauses for effect—"wasn't really invited."

And I was? "Why?" I ask.

"The prom queen competition is putting a strain on our friendship," Taylor confides. "I feel the need to branch out a bit and spend some time with new friends. Like you."

We're not friends, Taylor.

I'm starting to get suspicious. What is Taylor's game? I narrow my eyes at her. "I don't understand. After my verdict on Worthy, I'm not exactly the most popular person to hang out with."

Taylor laughs. "As I always say, no publicity is bad publicity. Besides, showing a little compassion for the underdog always looks good."

Great. Now I'm the charity case who's going to help Taylor win the prom queen competition. *As soon as I finish my obligation to this prom committee, we're done.*

After picking up the gift certificates from various shops in the mall, Taylor insists we look at prom dresses just in case she finds something she likes better than the two possibilities she already owns. I really don't have the energy to argue and don't want to go home to my sad playlist, so I reluctantly agree.

A young blonde woman with a pink-striped name tag that reads "Tracey" rushes over to greet us. Her fringe boots slap the sides of her legs.

"I love your cold shoulder top," she gushes at Taylor. "Aaaaamazing."

I've never received this kind of interest from any sales clerk, but Taylor takes it all in stride, obviously used to the attention. I hang out beside a polka-dotted, headless mannequin wearing a white lacy swimsuit and try to be invisible.

"Can I help you find something special?" Tracey smiles at Taylor, completely ignoring me. I want to yell "No, thank you" and run out the door, but Taylor is not the least bit intimidated. She starts picking out various dresses and holding them out toward me.

"We're looking for a dress for her," Taylor says, pointing at me. "It's for prom."

"I told you I wasn't going," I hiss under my breath, but Taylor ignores me.

The saleswoman arches one perfect brow and looks up and down my figure. "The prom dresses are a little . . . picked over."

"I was afraid of that," Taylor says.

I back up a little more and bump into the mannequin, sending it wildly wobbling toward a big pile of tank tops. Frantically, I catch it around the waist and try to set it up straight again quickly before anyone notices. Tracey watches, hands on hips, until I am through wrestling with the mannequin, then says, "Okay. Let's see what we can do for you."

She bustles around the store with Taylor following along behind, calling out opinions. I stand waiting near the headless mannequin. Tracey comes back carrying a strapless fit-and-flare blue BB Dakota dress.

"I'm not sure this will fit. You are quite . . . " Tracey pauses, staring at my chest. Finally, she looks up at my face. "Petite."

Taylor nudges my side and says, "Just try it on. What could it hurt?"

We follow Tracey back toward the dressing room, and Taylor sits down on a shiny pink-striped couch to wait.

"I could take some measurements," Tracey offers, but I just shake my head and grab the dress. The sooner I get this over with, the sooner I can get rid of Taylor.

"Trust me. The dress is going to look great. You just need to wear it with confidence," Taylor says through the door.

Easy for her to say.

Ⓧ ♥ Ⓧ

I pull the dress over my head and turn around for her to zip it up. When I face the mirror again, I'm shocked. This is all wrong. The dress stretches across my top, making me look unbalanced. It shows way too much skin. All I can think about is Nikki. She would know if it was right or not.

"Hey, guess what?" Taylor calls out.

I open the door a crack and she steps to the opening, holding her phone out. "Wolfgang has a cousin at another school. I told him you guys should go to prom together."

"Definitely not going to happen," I say.

Taylor pushes the door open a little wider. "That one fits nicely. Turn around."

I spin around a little self-consciously.

"How does it feel? Not too tight, but tight enough?"

"Ummm." I am not sure what I am supposed to say.

She gives me a squinty look and I cough into my hand to pretend I was just choked up.

"Don't you think it's a little low cut?" I ask carefully.

She covers her mouth with her long, thin fingers and giggles like it's the most hilarious thing she's ever heard. "It's perfect, silly." She bends down to dig around in the shopping bag at her feet.

"Ohhh-kay," I say slowly, staring at my reflection in the mirror. I unzip the dress and let it fall to the floor. With an attention span shorter than a two-year-old's, Taylor goes back to the couch to wait for me to get dressed.

She taps at the screen of her phone, looking in vain for something, and talking at me through the closed dressing room door.

"I like hanging out with you," Taylor says. Ever the politician, she is throwing out compliments like candy in a parade. "A lot of the other girls are jealous. That's why I don't have that many really close friends."

I frown. Taylor is not my friend. This dress is not me. None of this is right. I pull on my jeans and sweater, then put the dress back on the hanger.

Taylor keeps talking outside the door. "It's crazy that people are saying Nikki Aquino has a chance at junior prom queen. All because of that stupid Worthy thing." She looks up when I open the door. "No offense."

I do take offense. I leave the dress hanging on the hooks in the dressing room and walk toward her. For the first time, I say what's actually in my head. "Why wouldn't she have a chance just like everyone else?"

"Let's face it, Linden. Nikki is like the cat videos on YouTube. She's entertainment, but no one is actually serious about her being queen," Taylor says. "She makes us feel better about ourselves."

My head hums. I lean into Taylor's beautiful face, nose to nose. "You are pretty, Taylor. But that's all you are. No one describes you as funny or loyal or smart. You're *just* pretty."

She stares at me like I've sprouted another head.

Now that I've started, I can't stop. "No one will ever

expect you to work hard or accomplish anything. All they are ever going to see is your beautiful exterior."

Taylor's mouth falls open.

"And you may think you're better than Nikki . . . or me . . . but the truth is I just feel sorry for you."

"You forgot the dress," the salesgirl says as I march out of the store.

"No," I yell back over my shoulder. "I changed my mind."

I sit on the bench outside Sephora until closing time. When Nikki comes out, I'm there waiting. She looks at me but doesn't say anything.

"I need a makeover. I heard you were the best," I say. She keeps walking, so I stand up and step in front of her.

She stops. "What are you doing?"

The babble that pours out of my mouth resembles nothing like what I want to say. "I wanted the best for you and I thought I was helping but I was so . . . " My voice trails off.

"Stupid." She fills in the blank.

"I was going to say wrong."

"That, too."

My chin quivers.

She looks at me a moment, then grabs my hand. We sit back down on the bench. "Talk to me," she says. "Tell me what you're thinking."

I try to find the right words. "Okay. Well, to start. You are always so sure of yourself. Of everything," I say. "And I wish I were more like you, but I'm not." As I say it, I realize the truth in the words.

"I'm not always as confident as you think," Nikki says. "Sometimes I doubt myself."

I reach out and smooth her hair back behind one ear. "Nobody can be strong all the time. Not even Nikki Aquino."

After a minute, she says, "Jake and I broke up."

"Because of Worthy?" I ask, shocked.

She shakes her head. "No, because of me. I didn't like myself when I was with Jake."

"I'm sorry," I say. "Not that you broke up, but for how it feels. I know. Alex and I broke up, too."

"I heard." She leans her head against my shoulder. "I thought you guys were great together."

"Thanks," I say, then mutter under my breath, "I thought we were, too."

Nikki sighs deeply. "I didn't vote for you on Worthy. I didn't vote at all."

My body relaxes next to her and the knot in my stomach releases. "I'm glad."

"What about the prom?"

"I'm not going."

Nikki stares at me in disbelief. "Are you serious? You've worked so hard."

"Are you going?" I ask, surprised at her reaction. "Even without a date?"

"Nothing is keeping me from it." The old Nikki is back with a vengeance, and I couldn't be happier to see her.

I pull in a deep breath and give her a wobbly smile. "We could go together."

"Now that," Nikki says, standing up and pulling me up off the bench, "is a very good idea. And you, girlfriend, are going to need a dress."

CHAPTER TWENTY-TWO

On the night of the prom, I come downstairs to see the dining room table set with china and crystal. Candles are lit and soft jazz is playing in the background. I see them before they notice me—holding hands, fingers entwined. My mom smiles at my dad and then giggles, tucking her hair behind one ear.

"Mom?"

She looks at me, startled. "You look lovely, sweetie."

"What's going on here?" I ask.

"Your dad and I just thought as long as both you and your brother were out for the evening, we would have a date night."

"Couldn't you at least wait until I left?" I ask, but it makes my heart feel good to see them together. Someone should be having a romantic evening.

"Is that a new dress?" my mom asks. "Turn around. Let me see."

There was no time for Nikki to make a creation just for me, and the prom dresses at the mall were few and far between. So we improvised with a lace bolero over an embroidered cami tulle dress. I feel like an itchy princess whose fairy godmother had a bad day.

After the obligatory twirl, I ask, "Is Rat already gone?"

My dad nods. "He left to go pick up Ever thirty minutes ago. You'll have to take some pictures of the two of them at the dance. He was too excited to pose for me."

"Which reminds me, stand over by the mirror." Mom picks up her camera and I pose for a few quick snaps. I can't help but think of another photographer across town who is taking pictures of a fifteen-year-old girl dressed like Belle. And her brother.

Don't think about Alex.

I hold up a hand to stop my mother from taking any more pictures. "Nikki's going to be here any minute."

My dad stands up and goes around the table, holding his hand out to my mom. "Would you like to dance?"

They both laugh.

"Oh, brother," I say, rolling my eyes. A honk from outside lets me know that Nikki's waiting for me. "I have to go. You guys have fun."

"You too," Dad says as he pulls my mom into his arms and spins her around the room.

$$\textcircled{X}\;\textcircled{\heartsuit}\;\textcircled{X}$$

I hear the music in the parking lot from the moment I open the car door. The parade of excited fashionistas walking toward the gym is impressive, but the glimpse of sparkle inside the windows is extraordinary. The huge round tables are draped in black, with glittery white bows tied around the edges.

"The decorating committee outdid themselves," I tell Nikki.

"Thanks. It looks pretty good, if I do say so myself."

I flip down the mirror on the visor to get one last check before I get out. Nikki's tutorials were on point. My eye makeup is flawless, with sparkly lids and black liner, but the thought of walking in without Alex by my side is reflecting darkly in my eyes. The makeup. The dress. The shoes. Everything about this feels wrong.

Even though I'm glad to be with Nikki, I can't shake the shadow of disappointment. I think of Alex again. I wish for that magic mirror from Beauty and the Beast so I could see what he's doing right now. His sister's mass is probably over by now and they must be starting the reception. I hope it is just as spectacular as Izzy hoped it would be.

"Let me see," Nikki says, leaning over to get a look in the mirror. She jabs one more bobby pin in my already crowded hair. "There. That should hold it. Do you want more hair spray?"

I shake my head. We both get out of the car and stand for a moment, smoothing dresses and patting updos. Nikki is wearing the dress she created and a sparkly tiara headband in her thick, dark hair. She looks incredible. My last-minute dress feels awkward and I tug at the sides. My stomach is flipping, but I try to ignore it.

"Walk in there with your head held high," Nikki says. "Remember, it doesn't matter what people said about either of us."

"Let's get this over with," I say, and follow Nikki toward the music.

Inside, the gym is dark except for the stage lights illuminating the band and the big photo booth in the corner. Mr. Landmann, my world history teacher, is talking to Mrs. Boggs, my Spanish teacher, underneath the basketball hoop draped with green and gold streamers.

Nikki doesn't even wait for an invitation. She goes straight out on the floor and starts dancing as if no one is watching. At first, I stand over against the wall. It feels familiar. Comfortable. Raylene dances by with Ross, wearing a yellow rose corsage on one wrist. She towers over him in her high heels, but he smiles up at her as though she's the only one in the room. This is one couple Worthy couldn't break up, and I'm happy for them. If only Alex and I had survived as well.

I also see my brother dancing with his girlfriend, Ever, over near the edge of the dance floor. He is smiling down at her in his oh-so-handsome tuxedo, and I think it must be wonderful to have someone look at you that way.

I don't want to, but I think of Alex yet again. My heart hurts.

The music slows and couples step closer, arms winding around each other's necks. Jake Edwards suddenly appears at my elbow. Not surprisingly, he looks incredibly handsome in his tuxedo, even though his shirt is unbuttoned at the neck and his bow tie is dangling off to one side.

"Hey," he says.

I'm not sure why he's talking to me, but I nod back.

"Nikki looks great, doesn't she?" he asks, his eyes following her.

"She's beautiful," I say. "But then, she's always been beautiful. Too bad you couldn't see that."

"Yeah," he says quietly. We both watch Nikki, smiling and twirling around the room with Chance Lehmann. They get just close enough that we can hear her laugh at something Chance says; then they spin back out of sight into the crowd.

"I'm an idiot," Jake mumbles, and for a minute, I actually feel sorry for him. But before I can say anything else, he walks away and disappears into the crowd.

Wolfgang two-steps by me, spinning Taylor in his arms, then smoothly guides her around the perimeter of the dance floor. The prom queen votes were all turned in at the ticket booth when everyone came through the door, so Taylor has no more reason to play nice. She shoots me a dirty look, but I survive. I don't feel anything but relief that our fake friendship is over.

Jayla sees me and waves, threading her way through the dancing couples to my side. She's wearing a strapless porcelain ball gown and her skin is glowing. "I'm glad you came," she says. "You deserve the recognition for this great turnout."

I swallow hard and give her a hug. She knows the prom queen votes have been turned in, too, but she's still being nice. "You look amazing."

She grins and nods. "I know, right?"

Then Derek comes by and grabs her hand, dragging her away from me to the dance floor. "I'll see you later," she calls back over her shoulder.

The music slows down and Nikki comes back from dancing, face flushed and breathing hard. She taps me on the shoulder. "Let's get some punch."

Behind me, I hear two girls talking. I glance over my shoulder, but I don't know them.

"You know who is totally worthy? Melinda Billingsly and Jeff Keenan."

"They aren't even a couple and besides, that's not how it works."

"Maybe Worthy can make them a couple. Take this thing to a new level. I think they'd be perfect together."

"What are you talking about? They're both like the biggest dorks on the planet. Her science project is about creating some cure for cancer and he's totally into comic books. He dresses like a different superhero every day. Last week he was Aquaman."

"That's why it works. Don't you see? Worthy means they deserve each other. It's a class system. Geeks with geeks. The Lovelies with the Lovelies. Melinda Billingsly and Jeff Keenan are totally worthy of each other."

"Two wrongs make a right?"

"Exactly."

Nikki and I look at each other and exchange eye rolls. Nikki heads for the punch table and I turn to follow her.

"Would you like to dance?" Max Rossi is suddenly in front of me, blocking my view of the dance floor. "As long as you're not expecting me to live up to that." He nods toward Taylor and Wolfgang.

I laugh. "You obviously haven't seen me dance."

"Yes, I have. Remember when you took those tap-dancing lessons? I think you were about six."

"I totally forgot about that. I quit after two months. My mom was furious at the tap shoe investment. I think they are still in my closet somewhere."

"I remember."

"You remember a lot more than I do," I say.

Max smiles. He takes my hand and I let him lead me onto the dance floor.

Unfortunately, the music slows, so I have to move in closer. Max looks uncomfortable, but I don't know why. Maybe his shirt is too tight around his neck.

"I'm really sorry about the Worthy thing," he says.

I stiffen. I don't want to talk about Worthy.

"It's just . . . " He stumbles over the words, avoiding my gaze. "I never meant to hurt you."

"You didn't hurt me," I say quietly. "Worthy did."

Max looks down at the floor, not at me, but his feet keep moving slowly to the music. I know that look. It is the same look he had when we were nine and he wrecked my bike.

"Max, what did you do?" I ask slowly. The song keeps playing, but I stand stock still in the middle of the dance floor. He pulls me over to the wall, out of the way of the rest of the dancers.

He talks fast. "It was just a silly experiment at first. I wanted to learn how to develop an app to gather some simple feedback. Like, should we have more fruit in the cafeteria? Yes or no?"

"You created Worthy?" I can't believe it. I clench my hands to keep them from trembling. "*Why?* Why would you put everyone up for inspection?"

"I didn't know it would become such a big deal." He puts his hands on my shoulders. "You have to believe me."

It still isn't sinking in. But now I remember all those summer computer classes Max took when everyone else was on break.

"Why are you telling me this now?" I ask, as it all starts to sink in.

"I have to tell someone."

I close my eyes briefly. When I open them, all I can see is Max. His eyes are all soft and needy. I take a shaky breath. "How did you pick us? The couples, I mean."

"Well, obviously I started with Liam and Taylor because they were so perfect." He stops to look around, then continues, talking really fast. "Then I started trying other options. It was just random."

My mouth falls open and I hold a hand up to stop him. "You ruined people's lives . . . *randomly*?"

Max blinks. "When you say it like that, it sounds horrible. I never meant to hurt anyone."

"But why *me*, Max?" I can barely choke out the words. "We've always been friends."

Max makes a face. "Everyone thinks I'm a good friend. I hate that word. *Friend*. It's the worst word ever, and girls say it with this little inflection in their voice like it's the word *sorry*. They think I'm a buddy, a pal, Mister Nice Guy. I don't want to be your *friend*, Linden."

I don't care that people are gathering out on the dance floor, chattering excitedly and waiting for Kristen Fulton, the current student council president, to step up to the microphone. I don't care that the band is doing a drumroll to build suspense for the big announcements.

In the twinkling lights, Max actually looks apologetic. "You have to believe me, Linden. I never meant to hurt you."

I shake my head. He just doesn't get it. "But hurting other people is okay? I can't talk to you now, Max. I have to go."

I stumble away from Max. I hear him calling my name but I ignore him. I head toward the bathroom, my head reeling from the conversation. There are two girls at the sink. They look up from their phones and stare like I am some kind of space alien, mouths open and slack. I glare back at them and they scatter for the door.

Outside, I can hear Kristen's voice over the microphone. "Before we get to the queen and king announcements, I just want to thank all of you for dressing up in your finest and coming out to dance the night away on this magical, enchanted evening."

There's applause and some whoops from the crowd.

I stare at my reflection in the mirror. Everything feels heavy—the makeup, the dress, the hair. Layers upon layers. Like a princess turned into a beast by a magical spell, I can't see past the ugly created by other people's judgment. All of this heartache and self-doubt was because of Max Rossi's stupid experiment. I want to shout it from the rooftops. I want to go out there and scream it into the microphone.

"Special thanks to the junior class organizing committee, led this year by Heather Middleton. Heather, come on up here . . . "

More applause. I frown at myself. I don't want to be afraid of taking risks anymore. I don't want to watch from the sidelines—safe and alone. I am the only one who has the power to make myself feel unworthy, and I am the only one who can change it.

I dart outside and head to my locker, retrieving my gym bag. There are jeans and a white T-shirt inside. Back inside the bathroom, I kick off my silver sandals and pull the dress up over my head. It lies in a pile of shimmer on the white tile floor of the stall, and I stand there in my underwear looking at it for a moment. A small twinge of guilt at the thought of Nikki's hard work makes me scoop it up off the floor and put it into the bag at my feet. I pull on the jeans. Then the T-shirt. I don't have any other shoes, so I put the sandals back on even though they look strange with the jeans. I zip the bag up like a body bag being zipped up over a corpse.

My hair comes down much easier than it went up. I brush it back away from my face with spread fingers, searching for bobby pins and tangles. Digging around in my gym bag, I pull out a comb and work it through the hair-sprayed snarl of curls until it lies flat against my shoulders. I look in the mirror at my carefully made up face. My smoky Urban Decay eye shadow. The slight cat eyeliner that took me three tries to get right. The hint of blush. Winter's Blush lip stain. I pull out a paper towel and wipe at the corner. My lips smudge. I wipe harder and the lip stain only smudges more, slashing the red across the side of my mouth. I am a very sad clown.

The bathroom door creaks open.

"Are you all right?" Nikki stands beside me. Her reflection in the mirror is worried. "They're looking for you. It's almost time for the awards ceremony."

"Yes," I say. "I'm good."

"Okay," she says, but it's obvious she doesn't believe me.

I try to explain. "I've been good all along, I just didn't know it."

"I knew it."

"Thank you," I say quietly. "But you couldn't do it for me. I love you, Nikki, but I need to walk out there without you."

She nods.

"I don't want to hide behind things anymore. Not this dress. Not this makeup. Not you."

Beside the sink, the liquid soap is pink and institutional. I stare at it a few minutes, then pump it into my hand. Again. Again. I turn on the faucet to full blast and put my hands under the water, rubbing them frantically until the soap starts to foam. Then I lower my head down to the sink, washing and washing. The water runs red over my hands, rinsing away the lipstick and blush. I look back up to the mirror, and now my eyes are smudged thick black shadows. I can't tell if it is the water or the tears that make the long drips of black, and it doesn't really matter. They are both necessary now.

Instead of answering, Nikki pulls a paper towel out of the wall dispenser and hands it to me. "You got a little smudge on your face," she says.

I can't help it. I laugh. She laughs. We both laugh.

I wash my face until the water runs clear as glass under my hands. There is one more thing I need to do. I pull my phone out of my purse and send a text to Kat.

ME: MAX ROSSI IS BEHIND WORTHY

KAT: GOT IT

Then I hear Heather Middleton calling my name from the stage.

"Linden Wilson? Linden? Come on up here . . . "

When I walk out of the bathroom, heads turn and people talk. I keep going toward the stage and the microphone. I've found my voice and I'm going to use it.

Heather takes a step back, looking at me like I've grown two heads. I reach for the microphone. There is complete silence on the dance floor, everyone frozen in place with eyes locked on me.

"Hi. I'm glad everyone's having such a great time," I say, scanning the room. "And I also want to say . . . " I stop and take a deep breath. Nobody moves. "You can be anything you want tonight. Pretty. Brave. Popular. Smart. Funny. Talented."

I clear my throat. "Or none of those things. You are the one who decides. Not some app. Not a vote. No one else," I say. I see Max standing back by the refreshments table, staring at me. He rubs the back of his neck and his shoulders slump. I add one last thing. "Tonight I'm just going to be me. And that is enough."

I see Nikki standing in the back of the room by herself. She grins and gives me two thumbs up. The crowd parts as I step off the stage and make my way back to her. The music starts up again, louder than before, and everyone goes back to dancing.

"I'm leaving now," I tell Nikki. "I need to borrow your car. Can you get a ride home?"

She nods. I hold my palm out toward her in our

super-secret best friend salute, and she holds out hers to touch fingers.

I turn to go and head outside. Then I look back through the windows. I see Nikki going straight up to a gorgeous senior standing on the side of the dance floor. I watch his face—surprised at first, then smiling. She leads him out on the dance floor.

I smile, too, and then I turn and head for the car.

CHAPTER TWENTY-THREE

The room is packed with round tables full of people—
young and old. I slip in the back door and lean against
the wall, blending into the crowd. The band is playing
an old favorite, "Celebration," as kids in fancy dresses
and black dress pants run around the tables, playing tag
in the crowd. Older guests mingle, greeting and hugging
each other enthusiastically.

"*Buenas noches*," a white-haired gentleman exclaims as
a willowy, red-haired woman approaches. "When did you
get in?"

The woman squeezes his arm and leans in to kiss his
cheek. "We just drove up from Brownsville this morning.
Su sobrina luce preciosa."

I know *sobrina* means niece, so I think this must be
Isabella and Alex's uncle. He beams with pride at the com-
pliment. "She does look beautiful, doesn't she?"

A younger man joins the group carrying a toddler in a
pink tutu. "You haven't met my husband," the red-haired
woman says. "This is Jack and our daughter, Emma."

The men shake hands and then the older man holds his arms out to the little girl. *"Ay, que linda."*

The little girl shakes a head full of red curls and buries her face in her dad's shoulder. "She's shy," says the mother.

I know how she feels, but unfortunately there's no familiar shoulder for me to hide my face in. Shouts of recognition and bursts of laughter overwhelm the music as groups of people settle in at the elaborately decorated tables. I scoot back a little further against the wall. The red-haired woman glances over and smiles at me. She's probably trying to figure out if she knows me because everyone in this crowded ballroom seems to know everyone else.

The song ends, and a heavily made up woman steps into a spotlight at the side of the stage. She taps the mike to get everyone's attention, but it takes several tries before the crowd quiets enough for her to say it again.

"If I can have your attention . . . " she says. "We're about to begin our presentation."

Gradually, the noise subsides and the lights dim. I look around and see Alex across the room, talking to the other attendants. Standing beside the line of young couples waiting to go onstage, he looks very handsome in his tuxedo. I go completely still, my heart thudding in my chest.

The emcee continues at the microphone. "It's time now to present our court."

Everyone applauds. The woman at the mike gestures to the waiting pairs to begin parading around the dance floor.

"Mr. John Garcia is escorting Miss Cristina Salinas!"

Each couple strolls together, arms linked, until they reach the edge of the dance floor. The boys wear tuxes and yellow satin ties and the girls are in blue cocktail dresses with matching yellow sashes.

"Mr. Steven Lopez is escorting Miss Alexis Arroyo! Mr. Arturo Valdez is escorting Miss Shelly Lee Martinez!"

A photographer steps in front of them and snaps pictures of the couples as they parade around the stage.

"*Aplausos, por favor!* Don't they look lovely?"

The crowd claps again as the couples eventually take their seats in the chairs lining the back of the stage. One yellow taffeta-draped chair sits empty stage center, directly under the spotlight, waiting for the guest of honor. The lights in the ballroom dim. Drumroll. Then the band begins to play soft music in the background.

The emcee's voice lowers. "At this time, we will watch our quinceañera grow into the beautiful young woman she is becoming."

A PowerPoint presentation begins on the big screens on either side of the stage. The first photo to pop up shows Isabella as a baby building a sand castle at the beach. Others follow. A field trip to the zoo with her kindergarten class. Shooting a winning goal at a soccer match. Blowing out ten candles on her birthday cake. And more. Each photo shows her older and more confident. The last one lingers on the screen—a picture of Alex and Izzy facing the camera, his arm thrown around her shoulders. The proud grin on his face brings an instant lump to my throat. I've missed that look.

Finally, the announcer clears her throat one final time and leans in to put her scarlet lips close to the microphone. "Ladies and gentlemen, the moment we have all been waiting for. Will everyone please rise and join me in a big round of applause for our beautiful and lovely quinceañera— Isabella Maria Rivera, who is making her debut into society!"

Isabella and her mother stand together in the spotlight. Izzy's hair is elaborately curled and she is wearing a sparkling tiara. Her dress is bright yellow with gathered ruffles on the huge, full skirt. A perfect replica of Belle. The crowd cheers as her mother leads Isabella out on the dance floor toward the waiting chair. Her skirt, which is lifted by multiple petticoats, is so massive that her mother has to help her balance and ease her into the seat. Her mom's eyes fill up with tears and she wipes them away; then she backs away to leave Isabella sitting alone in the spotlight to the roar of applause.

Now it is Alex's stepfather, Sam's, turn. He walks slowly into the spotlight, obviously nervous, his head lowered. Isabella hands him a porcelain doll she had clutched to her side, and he gives her a bouquet of red roses in exchange. Then he kneels in front of her to swap out her flats for a pair of beautiful rhinestone-encrusted heels. The symbolism is clear and the significance brings a lump of emotions to my throat. Her childish toys and shoes are gone. The little girl has completed her transformation into a woman, with all the complexities and nuances this new, overwhelming status will bring.

The emcee steps back to the mike. "We wish you the best of luck, and may God bless you." The crowd stands and roars their approval, calling out, "We love you, Izzy!" as glasses are lifted in toasts all around the room. A glass is pushed into my hand, and suddenly everyone is clinking my glass to theirs as though I belong here.

After the toast, I stand in the crowd around the dance floor and watch Alex dance with his sister in the spotlight, circling the dance floor in a graceful waltz. He smiles down at her with such pride it makes my eyes brim with tears. If this were indeed a fairy tale and I were some kind of fairy godmother, I would grant her the wish of understanding her worth. But I know she's going to have to figure that out on her own.

Abuela Maria and Mrs. Annie Florence are the first to see me. I hold out my hand, but Alex's grandmother ignores it and pulls me in for a hug. I'm startled, but am able to choke out, "Good to see you" before being smushed against her chest.

When she finally releases me, she says, "I know Alex will be so happy you came."

I hope you're right.

Mrs. Annie Florence just nods and grins at me, her gray curls bobbing wildly on top of her round body. Neither of them says anything about the way I'm dressed.

"Linden?" Alex looks at me, his gaze steady. My heart is pounding so hard I think it might jump right out of my chest. I want to tell him I'm sorry for caring what other people think, and that he looks incredible, and to explain why I'm really underdressed. But I can't say any of that with his grandmother and her friend hovering, so I just say, "It was a beautiful ceremony."

"Yes, it was." He is still staring directly into my eyes, as though he can't believe I'm actually here, and I can't look away either. Finally, he asks, "Who won prom queen?"

"I don't know. I left before they announced it."

His eyebrows rise in surprise. "Why? Weren't you supposed to get some kind of award?"

"It wasn't important anymore. I'm through trying to be some other version of myself. This is who I am."

"And I like who you are."

My whole body relaxes in relief. This is all I need to hear.

He holds out his hand. "Want to dance?"

I nod and put my hand in his, watching his fingers intertwine and tighten around mine. But by the time we walk out onto the dance floor, the slow song ends, and "The Chicken Dance" starts up. He looks at me questioningly, and I laugh. I don't care what we dance to, I'm just so freaking happy to be here.

CHAPTER TWENTY-FOUR

The party is winding down. After enthusiastic good-byes, families have gathered up sleepy children and trickled out, leaving just Izzy and her friends left to dance the rest of the night away.

Alex and I sit at an empty table strewn with half-filled glasses and tangled streamers, watching the girls. Isabella has changed into a short bright-purple dress much more suited to dancing and is currently jumping around wildly with her two besties—their hands waving in the air to the music.

I look over at Alex. His jacket is hanging on the back of his chair. His crisp white dress shirt is untucked and unbuttoned at the neck. I can't help it. I have to touch him. Leaning over, I brush his thick black hair back off his forehead, my fingers lingering as they slide down his face. I feel the muscles in his cheek move under my hand as he smiles. Then he turns his head and his lips are on my palm. The heat explodes into my cheeks.

"Let's go for a walk," Alex says, his voice soft and deep.

"Yes," I say, although it really wasn't a question. I scoop

up my satchel from under the table and follow him out into the foyer. Alex picks up a flashlight from the entry table and leads me out onto the big wraparound porch.

"Where are we going?" I ask.

"It's a surprise. You'll see." He leads the way down the front steps and along a small path, his shiny black dress shoes crunching on the pine-needle-covered ground. When the light from the party behind us is blocked by the trees, he flips on the flashlight and reaches back for my hand in the dark.

After a few hundred feet, the gravel path turns to dirt and narrows. He holds my hand and goes in front, leading the way through the trees. "Follow me. I'll show you. Look for the lights up ahead."

When I walk into the clearing, I gasp. It is lit by thousands of white lights draped from trees in glowing strands. Bouquets of green balloons are tied to the arms of two Adirondack chairs that sit side by side, and each balloon has one word printed on it with black permanent marker.

YES.

I blink hard, stunned. "You did all this?"

He nods.

"But how did you know I would see it?"

He shakes his head. "I didn't. Not for sure. But I was going to text you after the ceremony and ask you to meet me here. I hoped you'd come."

Logs are stacked in the stone fire pit, ready to be lit, and all the ingredients for s'mores wait on a nearby wooden table. Everything is just right. There is no feeling of racing toward finish lines and being second best. I reach out and trace a finger along the length of his arm.

"I'm glad I'm here."

"Me too." He sinks into the chair by the fireplace. A touch on his phone and John Legend's "All of Me" starts to play.

Breathe. Just breathe.

I put my bag down on the ground and sink into the chair beside him. He leans in to light the fire and it quickly flickers up into the dark.

When he looks at the bag in between us, he says, "Not exactly the standard accessory for prom."

"I went by my house on the way over here. I wanted to show you something." I reach down, open the flap, and pull out my laptop.

He frowns. "It's not more Worthy, is it?" he asks.

"No, it's not Worthy." I push the power button. The start-up screen glows.

Alex sighs. "I just thought if we ignored all the negative attention, it would go away, but I didn't see how much it was hurting you. I'm sorry."

"It's okay. I had some time to think this week . . . about Worthy and how I let it get inside my head. And I thought about you." I pause and take a breath. "And somehow all those thoughts got tangled up with Isabella's theme for tonight—Beauty and the Beast."

His eyebrows rise in question, but he lets me keep talking.

"So I wondered . . . " I lean in across the space between us, talking faster. "What if the beast never turns back into a prince at the end? Belle loved him when he was a beast. So, if the point of the story is that it's what's inside that matters, then he was good enough just like he was, right?"

Alex thinks for a minute, then nods slowly.

"So, I wrote a *new* story." I make a few clicks, then hand it carefully over to him. "And for the first time . . . well . . . " My voice trails off into the dark. I clear my throat, my heart hammering. "I want someone to read it."

He looks down at the screen, then back to me.

"I mean . . . " I stumble over the words. "I want *you* to read it."

"You finished it?" he asks, still not comprehending.

I nod. "I'm going to send it in to the contest."

"And I get to read it?

I nod again. My laugh is shaky, thanks to my nerves.

"Are you sure?" he asks, looking over at me incredulously. I sit with my arms wrapped around my knees. Even though the thought terrifies me, I've never been more sure of anything.

"Yes," I say. "Finally."

His eyes are already tracking the words across the screen, but he says to me, "Want to make us a s'more? I know it's not exactly a fancy dinner in front of a lot of people . . . "

"I don't care about impressing other people anymore." I slip off my high-heeled sandals and stretch my bare feet out toward the heat of the fire. "This is exactly what I want."

"Good," he says, but his eyes don't leave the screen. He keeps reading, but he takes my hand in his, entwining our fingers. We sit like that, holding hands while he continues to read, smiling sometimes at the words I wrote. I look at the fire, biting the inside of my lip, and wait nervously. When he finishes, he sighs, closes the computer, and puts it down on the table next to him.

He leans in until the tip of his nose touches mine, and I feel the tingle all the way down my spine. "I knew it would be wonderful," he says. "And it was."

I let out a breath I didn't even know I was holding.

Then he smiles and gets to his feet, opening his arms wide. I walk into them, barefaced and barefoot, to enjoy one more slow dance under a night full of stars.

Max Rossi & the Huntsville High Hornets

IS HE WORTHY?

The secret is out, peeps! Max Rossi is the mastermind (if you can call it that) behind Worthy. So maybe we should give him a little taste of his own medicine?

Here's what you are saying:

* Ha! Whoever did this gets my vote!

* I'm not voting for him here or anywhere

The vote is in . . .

Stay tuned . . .

100% of you say MAX ROSSI is NOT WORTHY!!!

As of today, the Worthy app will no longer be active. We recommend deleting it from your phone to free up space.

THE HORNET

- SAT tests next week. Check the revised testing schedule for start times.
- Congratulations to our junior-senior prom queens! Senior prom queen—Briella Davis. Junior prom queen—Jayla Williams. Check out the prom photo-booth pics online now!
- Congratulations to Linden Wilson, who won the 13th Annual Marty Speer Literary Prize for Young Writers contest, presented by the *Thompson Review*! Her short story, "Enough," will be published on the journal's website. In addition, she will receive a full scholarship to the *Thompson Review* Young Writers Workshop in Austin, Texas, this summer.
- Good luck in the playoffs to the boys' baseball team!
- The elections results are in! Our next student body president will be Emma Johnson!
- Are you **CRUSHING** on someone? Want to tell them anonymously to see if they like you, too? Check out this HOT NEW app—**CRUSH**—just for Huntsville High School students! Everybody who's anybody is going to be talking about this tomorrow! Don't be left out. Free download *HERE*.

ACKNOWLEDGMENTS

First of all, thank you for reading. I hope you know you are worthy. Of love, beauty, ambition, laughter, dreams, and everything your heart desires.

So many people helped in writing this book, but most especially my editor, Aimee Friedman. Her editorial skills are only matched by her kindness. My deepest gratitude and respect also goes to my agent, Sarah Davies, at Greenhouse Literary Agency for her passion, professionalism, and persistence. I am continually amazed by her unwavering faith in me. Huge thanks also to everyone at Scholastic who made this book, and my dream of becoming an author, a reality, especially David Levithan, Sheila Marie Everett, Tracy van Straaten, Lizette Serrano, Lauren Festa, Rachel Feld, Yaffa Jaskoll, Kerianne Okie, Olivia Valcarce, and so many more.

I'm blessed to have so many writing friends who always share encouragement and cheer me on even when the words don't appear: Kathi Appelt, Debbie Leland, Katy

Longshore, Talia Vance, Bret Ballou, Kristen Held, Beth Hull, Robin Fitzsimmons Meng, and Veronica Rossi. My heartfelt thanks to Karen Rattenborg for her traveling companionship and Greg Rattenborg for supporting her as my unofficial PR director. Thank you also to my university colleagues and friends who support this dream in countless ways. Thanks in particular to Derek Decker, Wendy Fothergill, Jody Drager, Juliana Searle, Rod Lucero, Karmen Kelly, and Heidi Frederiksen. Writing a book is a mental exercise, so I'm very grateful to Jorine Peterson, Justin Thompson, and the whole "Old People's Crossfit" gang who constantly challenge me to balance my writing brain with a few burpees.

As always, deep gratitude to my family for their unconditional love and support. Extra recognition to my husband, Jay Gines, for the cooking, the cleaning, the laundry, and everything else that holds our life together when I disappear into the writing cave. I love you. Forever and ever, Amen.

Finally, I miss you mom. Every. Day.

ABOUT THE AUTHOR

Donna Cooner is the acclaimed author of *Skinny* and *Can't Look Away*. A Texas native and graduate of Texas A&M University, Donna currently lives in Fort Collins, Colorado, with her husband, a cat named Stu, and two chocolate Labradors, Roxanne and Murphy. Follow @donnacooner on Twitter or visit her online at donnacooner.com.